TRILOGY NO. 106
NICE & NAUGHTY
CAT JOHNSON

TRILOGY NO. 106: NICE & NAUGHTY

Published by Linden Bay Romance, 2006
Linden Bay Romance, LLC, U.S.
ISBN Trade paperback:
978-1-60202-009-2   1-60202-009-4
ISBN MS Reader (LIT):
978-1-60202-008-5   1-60202-008-6
Other available formats (no ISBNs are assigned):
PDF, PRC & HTML

Cover art by *Beverly Maxwell*

Dedicated to firefighters everywhere

SECRET RECIPE

Chapter 1

"I can't do this."

Her voice came through the cell phone crystal clear. Didn't that just figure? Cell reception was usually crappy at best, but now that his girlfriend of nearly two years was dumping him…yup, clear as a bell.

Scott O'Malley sighed and ran one hand over his newly shorn hair. "Linda, can we talk about this later? Please?"

He felt the towel wrapped around his waist start to slip and grabbed for it with his free hand. As if getting dumped wasn't bad enough, the fact that he was naked and in a room full of fellow firefighters at the time of the dumping was just icing on the cake.

"There's nothing to talk about. I've packed all the stuff you left at my apartment in a box. I'll leave it outside my door so you can pick it up."

"O'Malley! You're up!" Scott glanced over as one of the guys from his firehouse summoned him.

Linda wanted to play games, he could play games. "Fine. I'll be over after I'm done here. Oh, and Linda, make sure my Ladder Company No. 3 t-shirt is in the box."

He heard her hesitate. "Um…I will."

Ha! If she didn't want him anymore, she sure as hell couldn't have his shirt, too bad if it was her favorite thing to sleep in every night. Not feeling as petty as he knew he should, Scott flipped the phone shut and realized there was no pocket in which to put it away. One of the hazards of wearing nothing but a scrap of terrycloth, he guessed.

"You okay?" His friend and fellow firefighter Troy O'Donnell was suddenly next to him.

"Yeah. Fine." He shoved the cell phone at Troy, as if the phone was at fault for the dumping rather than his girlfriend—make that former girlfriend. "Put this somewhere for me, will ya?"

Troy nodded. "Sure."

And now, on to the day's next humiliating event...

1

Troy's sister Tessa, the very cute and equally off-limits photographer—Troy had invoked the sister-rule—stepped up to Scott. She thrust one hand in his direction, camera held in the other. "Scott?"

He made sure to hold the towel with one hand as he shook hers with the other. "Yup. Where do you want me?" Realizing that sounded inadvertently suggestive, he amended his offer. "Um, to pose, I mean."

She smiled. "Well Mr. July, would you feel comfortable standing next to the barbecue grill wearing just this?" Draped over her arm was an apron that read, "Kiss the Cook."

"Just that?" He eyed the item and tried to estimate exactly how much of him it would cover.

She tilted her head to one side. "Only if you're all right with it. If not, we'll come up with something else."

He shrugged. What the hell, he was now totally single, unattached and available. Why not be practically nude in a calendar that would be seen by literally thousands of single girls throughout the city. "No problem."

Whistles and applause ensued as Scott tied the apron around his waist and whipped off the towel. The front of him was covered, but the rear view definitely was not. He sidled his way over to the grill, keeping his butt facing away from Troy's sister, which meant he flashed all of the other firemen in the room.

Oh, well. They were all in this endeavor together, and the *Hunky Firemen* calendar was to benefit a good cause, the local children's hospital. Getting photographed naked for charity was so *not* what he thought he'd be doing when he took the firefighter's test.

Antonio Sanchez, who had the honor of being Mr. October in the calendar and had held nothing but a pumpkin in front of himself, handed Scott a large spatula. "Here. It helps if you have something to hold onto."

"Thanks." Since Scott had a nearly irresistible urge to keep both of his hands clamped tightly over the apron covering his you-know-what, the prop definitely helped keep at least one hand otherwise occupied. If he only had something to keep his mind equally occupied so he wouldn't remember that after this photo shoot, he'd be picking up what remained of his relationship with Linda, and it fit into a single cardboard box. Wasn't that sad.

A few dozen photos and forced smiles later and Scott was done posing. It was quicker and easier than he'd thought it would be, nudity aside, and he had nearly forgotten his misery. But now, he had no further reason to procrastinate. He realized the time had come to go collect his box. Oh, goody.

He grabbed the towel from where he'd ditched it. Bare butt safely covered again, he made his way back to where he'd left his clothes in the studio's dressing room and found Troy already there.

As Mr. December, Troy had gotten to wear actual pants in his photos. That had made Scott a little envious, although the fight between the O'Donnell siblings over the pants vs. no pants issue had been pretty amusing. Tessa had wanted Troy in nothing but a strategically placed Santa hat. Lucky for Troy he proved to be the more stubborn O'Donnell. He won the standoff and got to wear fire pants, but with no shirt.

Scott noticed Troy glance over as he grabbed his shirt off the bench. "We're not on shift again until tomorrow so a few of us are going out for a beer. You wanna come?"

Scott's mouth twisted. "I have to stop by Linda's." He sat down heavily on the bench and rubbed his hands over his face, suddenly very tired.

Troy paused, his shirt in his hand. "What's up? You've been weird since that phone call."

"Linda dumped me. On the phone, after almost two years."

Troy frowned. "Just like that? Out of the blue. Why?"

"I got the ultimatum last night." *Marry me or it's over*, she'd demanded. Apparently, judging from today's phone call, *I'm not ready, I need more time* was not a good enough

3

answer for Linda.

Troy groaned as Antonio joined them in the dressing room. "What're you groaning about?"

"Scotty got the ultimatum."

Antonio winced. "Ah, man. And?"

"And can we swing by and get my box full of stuff off Linda's front doorstep on the way to the bar?"

Wasn't that ironic? His and Linda's relationship came down to two boxes, a small velvet box containing a diamond engagement ring or a large cardboard one containing his stuff. What a deceptively simple concept. Most men assumed relationships were complicated, but not really. When you got right to it, everything boiled down to two options: choose box number one or box number two. Easy.

Antonio gave him a sympathetic smile. "Sure we can stop. I'll even get out of the car and get your stuff for you so you don't have to have the usual post-ultimatum confrontation."

"And I'll buy the first round of shots when we get to the bar. I'm thinking this situation calls for a visit from our old friend Jose Cuervo."

Scott couldn't help but smile at them both. "Thanks, guys." A barroom full of testosterone and free-flowing tequila, that was the quickest remedy he knew of for a broken heart and a bruised ego. Sure, tomorrow he'd have to deal with a hangover and the gaping hole in his life, but for tonight, it was all good.

A few hours later, Scott leaned on the bar and laughed when his elbow slipped off. He caught himself with his other hand. "You know what? This is all I need, just my buddies...and maybe another beer."

"Another beer here!" Troy called out to the bartender, holding onto the bar rail as he swayed a bit.

"You're better off without her, anyway. Once this calendar hits, we won't be able to beat the girls off with a stick!" Gordy, Mr. February, slurred. He'd gotten to hold a really big red heart-shaped box—the kind that chocolate came in at Valentine's Day—in front of his family jewels for his photos. Although, when you're naked, can the box ever be big enough?

"Jeez, don't say that! That's exactly what I'm afraid of." Troy grimaced over Gordy's comment as he delivered Scott's beer.

"Why? What's wrong with you? Over at our house, the great Troy O'Donnell from Ladder 3 is legendary when it comes to the ladies." Big and burly Gordy was borrowed from Engine Company 31 since some genius had decided the calendar should contain only unmarried naked firemen. Although the calendar was Ladder 3's initial idea, they'd had to hit three other firehouses to find enough single and willing guys to fill the twelve months.

But it was good getting to know the other men better, and after tonight's male bonding debauchery, Scott felt like they were all brothers in arms in the battle of the sexes, no matter which house they belonged to.

Antonio laughed. "That is the problem, Gordy. Troy's engaged now, but his fiancé doesn't know she's marrying the former Casanova of the city's firefighters."

"And she's not going to know either," Troy added with a warning in his voice.

Antonio shook his head. "I don't know what you're worried about, man. Amy wouldn't care. That was before you ever met her. You were just waiting for the right girl, that's all."

Gordy leaned in. "So come on, O'Donnell, tell me the truth. Is it true you hit triple digits?"

Troy shot him a less than brotherly look. "No comment."

Scott took another slug of beer. "How did you know, Troy? How did you know that girl number one-nineteen was *the one*, when the first one-hundred-eighteen weren't?"

"One-hundred and nineteen! Jesus, O'Donnell. You are my new idol."

Troy ignored Gordy's outburst. "You just know, Scotty, with no question. If you're having doubts about Linda, then she's not the one for you."

Antonio rolled his eyes. "As if you should be giving relationship advice. I seem to remember I had to convince you that Amy wasn't a lesbian!"

"Whoa! She was a lesbian?" Gordy nearly dropped his beer.

Troy scowled. "No, but at the time I thought…oh, just shut up, Gordy. And *you* can step in with your own relationship advice for Scotty any time you feel like it, Antonio. You've been awfully quiet tonight except for when you're discussing my personal life."

Antonio scuffed his black cowboy boot on the grungy floor of the bar. "I didn't think Scotty'd want to hear much from me tonight after what happened with him and Linda. Before the shoot today, I, uh, stopped by the jewelers and ordered an engagement ring for Maddie."

Scott swung his gaze from Antonio to Troy, and then back again. "Jeez! You're getting engaged to your girlfriend now, too?"

Antonio shrugged. "I'm not asking her until New Year's Eve, but I couldn't wait any longer to order it."

Scott shook his head. "If both of you are getting married, maybe I'm wrong. Maybe I should just propose to Linda. It would be easier, I guess, than fighting about it."

Antonio shook his head. "No, man. Are you crazy? Troy's right, you'll know when you've found the right one. Don't jump into marriage just because everyone else is doing it."

Gordy chimed in. "Damn right. You'll end up right back where you are now, alone but with an ex-wife and only half your worldly assets instead of an ex-girlfriend and all your stuff in a box."

He sighed, knowing they were right. But that word, *alone,* stuck with him. Yup. The minute Scott left the bar that night he knew he'd feel alone, and fueled with beer and tequila, he'd call Linda. Then what? More fighting? Some make-up sex? An ill-fated marriage proposal…

He took the cell phone out of his pocket and slid it across the bar. "Somebody take that and don't let me use it to call Linda tonight, no matter what."

"Oh, yeah. Nothing worse than the drunk-dial to the ex," Gordy agreed as Antonio, probably the least drunk of them, picked up the phone and pocketed it.

Scott glanced around the group and realized he loved these guys, and then he realized something else. As far-gone as he was, it still struck him through his drunken haze that not one of them was sober enough to drive back to the firehouse. "You know what, guys? We forget to designate a driver."

They all looked at each other blankly for a moment.

"I guess I could call Maddie to come pick us up." Antonio squinted at his watch in the dim light of the neon beer sign and cringed. "Ugh, how did it get so late? She's definitely sleeping by now."

"We could try and get a taxi I guess," Gordy suggested.

Troy held up his hand. "Not to worry. I have a much better solution." He whipped out his cell phone and called out to the bartender. "Hey, Ralph. Does the pizza place next door deliver?"

The bartender looked up from the beer he was pouring. "Yup, and it's free if they take more than thirty minutes."

"Perfect. What's the phone number?"

Ralph recited the number as Troy dialed and everyone watched. "Yeah, I'd like to order a large pizza to be delivered…"

Thirty minutes or less later, a confused pizza delivery boy pulled his crowded economy-sized car up in front of Ladder Company No. 3 and four drunken firemen with one piping hot cheese pizza piled out.

Scott looked around at the small group stumbling up the stairs of the firehouse and smiled. He had no inclination and no cell phone to call Linda, but he did have a bunk at the firehouse for the night, pizza to fill his belly and good friends. Life, at least for tonight, was good. He'd worry about tomorrow in the morning.

Chapter 2

"I'm very sorry but I can't do it."

"But you have to do it." Begging was not out of the question at this point.

"No, actually, I don't. Good luck finding someone, though." Then there was a click.

Lexi Cooper gripped the phone until her knuckles were white as panic started to set in. She glanced down at the yellow pages and the last number she'd dialed. *Zoey's Events*. That was it. She'd reached the Z's. There were no more listings. She'd called every caterer in a tri-state area and not one was available.

"What am I going to do?" she whispered to herself.

"Here's an idea, how about learn to cook," Robert suggested offhandedly from across her apartment.

She glared at him and his ridiculous suggestion. "As my agent, you are supposed to support me and solve problems like this. So start solving."

"As a self-proclaimed renowned lifestyle maven, you are supposed to know how to cater a simple fundraising event yourself." He raised a brow and let the accusation hang in the air.

Lexi rose out of the desk chair and planted both fists on her hips. "You created the monster I've become. I only wanted to write general lifestyle articles. You are the one that insisted I add entertaining and food to my column even though I can't cook. You are the one that arranged the cookbook deal. You are the one that said yes to the cable television cooking show. *You* created Lexi Cooper, queen of entertaining, not me!"

"And the cookbook deal and cable show pay for this very spacious apartment. If I remember correctly, you were more than happy to jump on this bandwagon. And, may I remind you that *you* were the one that announced you would help with the planning of the Hunky Firemen fundraising event, during a live television broadcast no less, not me."

She glanced up at the older, gray-haired man in his impeccable charcoal gray suit. Her deals had probably paid for that suit. Robert had as much to lose as she, so how could he be so calm? Lexi let out a long slow breath. "Well, what was I supposed to do? Say no to helping out with the biggest charity event of the year and look like a bitch for not supporting the city's bravest men and sickest children?"

Robert grabbed one of Lexi's hands and squeezed in a fatherly manner, finally showing her some support and acting like she presumed an agent was supposed to. But since he'd been her one and only agent since the very beginning, she wasn't exactly sure what other agents were like.

"You did the right thing, and you've done a great job. The fireman calendar is selling like hot cakes, thanks to your brainstorm of using only unmarried firefighters. The promotional idea—your idea—for the calendar men to play Santa Claus all over town the week before the bachelor auction, which was also your idea, is brilliant. And the cocktail party 'bachelor mixer' at Bryant's Department Store will raise a ton of cash and raise even more awareness for the children's hospital."

"Except that there will be no food for the guests to eat at the party. I wish I'd never come up with that last idea." Lexi sighed heavily.

"Alexis, I know you think I was just being a smart-ass, but I was serious about what I said before. I do think you should learn how to cook. You're smart, you're talented and you're eroding your own self-confidence by insisting you can't learn."

He was using her full name, which is what he always did when he coddled her, but this time it wasn't going to work. "I can't learn. I burn water!"

He shook his head. "I don't believe you. You do great on the cooking show."

"Because all I do is read a script from the teleprompter. All the final food is pre-prepared by the chef on the set because *you* told them I am too busy to do it myself. Which is the same excuse we are using about why I can't come up with hors d'oeuvres for five hundred for the Bryant's event without an outside caterer. Only in the middle of the holiday season, there's not a reputable caterer to be had anywhere. Christ, how does anyone even begin to cook for five hundred people?"

Robert was still silently watching her. He could be quiet better than anyone else she'd ever met. And dammit, it worked every time. She couldn't stand it. She had to fill the silence, so she gave in.

"All right. Let's say, just for the sake of argument, that I did want to learn. How the hell does Lexi Cooper explain that she needs basic cooking lessons? What do I do, go to the local trade school in disguise and enroll in Cooking 101?"

"We get you private lessons. Pay the instructor off with enough money, and enough legal threats, that she will never talk to the press, or anyone else, about the fact you can't cook. There's a great woman chef I know who would probably do it…"

"I don't do well with women." At Robert's raised brow she elaborated. "Why do you think I quit the PR agency and chose to be a writer? One toxic female boss too many, that's why. I work better independently anyway."

"Fine, we'll find you a man."

Lexi smiled as her mind took a turn for the gutter. Ha, if only Robert could perform that miracle and actually find her a man. It had been a long time…much, much too long.

As if he read her mind, he smiled. Damn, it was unnerving when he did stuff like that. Too bad the only man in her life who knew her this well was her married agent who was old enough to be her father's older brother. "I *meant* to teach you to cook."

Lexi scowled at his persistence when it came to this crazy idea, which she doubted would work and still didn't solve her problem. "The event is in a few weeks. It's doubtful I can learn to cook at all, but even if I can, I won't be up to speed in time to cater a fundraiser for five hundred."

Robert smiled patiently. "You'll come up with something. You always do." He pinched her cheek lightly, much like her granddad used to do when she was little.

She rolled her eyes at his unwavering confidence in her, secretly wishing she shared it. "I'm glad one of us thinks so."

~

Hitler was alive and well and teaching cooking to Lexi. At least, she was convinced it was him judging by the dictator-like attitude, insane outbursts and irrational demands of perfection. She'd been reduced to tears in the ladies' room more than once. He'd also thrown her own culinary creations, imperfect though they were, at her. She was beginning to wake up regularly in cold sweats after dreaming of such horrors as falling soufflés and curdled eggs.

And now it was midnight and she was, of all places, in the dairy aisle of the all-night convenience store. She had to practice her chocolate soufflé before tomorrow's torture session with Fredrick, gourmet chef from hell.

Neither looking right nor left, Lexi and her shopping cart rushed full-speed toward the egg carton display…and smashed, demolition derby style, directly into another wagon. The momentum nearly flung her head first into her own cart. As it was, the handle jabbed her in the stomach, knocking the wind out of her and leaving her gasping.

Then she looked up at the driver of the other cart and was breathless for a different reason.

"Are you all right?" Mr. Muscles in the firefighter t-shirt and jacket looked concerned.

Lexi managed to nod, but not much more than that.

"Where were you going in such a hurry anyway?" He raised a brow and looked back at her as he reached in…and took the last four cartons of eggs.

"I need those eggs!"

He glanced at the eggs, already planted securely in his cart and then back at her. He was polite but firm when he said in a no nonsense keep-away-from-my-eggs sort of way, "Sorry, so do I."

Handsome as the devil and with the muscles of Paul Bunyan or not, she was tired, frustrated—in more ways than one—and she needed those eggs. Not above flirting them away from him, Lexi unzipped the jacket of her sweat suit a bit more, thrust her chest out and said in her sweetest voice, "Surely you could spare a dozen or two. You can't possibly need all four dozen eggs."

The breast-thrust move worked as his eyes dropped. But then he raised them back up to her face again and smiled, shaking his head. "Sorry, but I need them all." He folded his massive arms across his chest and waited for the next offensive.

Unfortunately, she was out of moves and out of patience. She stamped one foot with frustration. "Why do you need them all? For what?"

That earned her an even bigger smile. "That was cute."

She fisted her hands on her hips. "What?"

"When you stamp your foot and pout with your hands on your hips like that, it's cute."

"Don't you pick on me, you...you...egg hog!"

At that, he laughed aloud. Finally, he wiped a hand over his mouth and sobered enough to explain. "Look. I'm sorry. It's obvious that you have some sort of attachment to these eggs. But I need all four dozen because I promised to feed a dozen hungry guys four-egg omelets in just a few hours."

Lexi reached into the refrigerated display case and grabbed a carton of egg substitute. "Here, use this. It's better for their cholesterol."

"I've got four pounds of bacon in this shopping cart. Do you really think they are worried about their cholesterol? Why don't *you* use the fake eggs?"

"Because I'm making soufflés." Her voice cracked on the last word and Lexi realized she was losing it...yet again. Why had she ever agreed to take cooking lessons? She told Robert she couldn't do it. She turned her head away before he saw her start to cry. "Never mind. They're all yours. I quit."

Abandoning the cart in the middle of the aisle, Lexi started walking away, until a strong hand on her arm and a deep voice stopped her. "No. Wait."

She stopped, but didn't turn around, and neither did he move his hand off her arm.

"You can have the eggs." The voice reverberated behind her.

"No. I don't need them any more. I quit. I'll never learn how to cook anyhow and I'm tired of killing myself trying." She wiped the tears quickly away so she could turn back to the magnanimous mystery man who was suddenly so willing to share his eggs with her. "Thanks anyway."

He watched her closely, his dreamy blue eyes, which contrasted so nicely with the dark wavy hair, narrowed. "You wanna go for a drink or coffee? Or maybe some fried eggs or something?" He smiled.

"Now?"

He nodded. "There's an all-night diner right down the street."

It was frightening how quickly she made up her mind, especially since she didn't even know his name. "I'd like that."

Chapter 3

"So let me get this straight. Your name is Alexis, but you won't tell me your last name. Originally, you desperately had to make a soufflé tonight, but now you don't. What are you, in some sort of culinary witness protection program?"

Scott didn't mention the fact that she'd also hesitated before giving him even just her first name. She was nervous, but at least she wasn't crying like she had been in the store.

He was happy when Alexis laughed and made a joke of her own. "Sorry. If I told you, I'd have to kill you."

He smiled back at her. What was it about this girl that made him want to help her? Must be the innate hero in him, the same instinct that had made him join the army and then after his tour was up, become a fireman.

"Seriously, though. You were reduced to tears in the middle of the dairy aisle over a few dozen eggs. I know we just met, but if you need to talk, I'm a good listener."

She looked up at him and then dropped her eyes, but not before he noticed them start to glisten. "Ah, jeez. I didn't mean to make you cry again. I'm sorry."

She shook her head and finally raised shiny eyes to meet his. "Don't be sorry. It's just that you're being so nice. I'm sorry. I can't handle that right now."

"You can't handle someone being nice to you?" He raised a brow.

She buried her face in her hands and let out a half laugh. "I'm really tired and under a lot of pressure right now. I'm a big mess and if you want to run away screaming, I won't blame you one bit."

Scott shook his head. "Don't worry, I'm not going anywhere. I don't scare so easily." He realized what he'd just said and it gave him pause. He had run screaming in fright when Linda had demanded a ring. But this girl wanted nothing more from him than a dozen eggs. He was sure that must be the difference.

Scott looked at the mystery girl in front of him. In the

few months since Linda had dumped him because of his inability to commit on the spot to a lifetime with her, he'd steered clear of all females. But the tearful egg confrontation with this woman had piqued his curiosity, not to mention his interest, on a personal level.

This Alexis No-Last-Name was quite a piece of work. If Linda had stamped her foot at him and pouted, he would have laughed her out of the store. But when Alexis did it, he'd had the urge to grab her and see if she tasted as sweet as she looked.

Wearing a plain sweat suit with not one bit of makeup on her face, she was still the sexiest thing he'd seen in a long time. He studied her more closely. Short brown curls, warm brown eyes. But something nagged at the back of his brain. Why did she seem familiar to him?

A sudden and extremely unappealing thought struck him. What if she was one of Troy's one hundred and nineteen and that's why he recognized her? Damn. She was exactly Troy's type, too. Petite but curvy in all the right places. Even engaged, the firehouse Casanova was still getting in the way of his dating life. Scott wasn't thrilled about accepting Troy's leftovers, but with over a hundred of them running around the neighborhood, the chances of encountering one was high. He supposed he had no choice in the matter, because even if Alexis was one of the many fish in Troy's sea, Scott didn't think that fact would be enough to make him want to throw her back.

He steeled his nerves and asked the dreaded question. Better to find out now rather than later. "This may be an odd question, but do you know Troy O'Donnell?"

She frowned. "No, I don't think so. Why do you ask?"

Ding, ding, ding. That was the correct answer. Scott smiled. "No reason. You'd remember if you knew him. So, during the recent battle of the eggs, you mentioned learning to cook…" He paused as Alexis started to look really uncomfortable.

"Did I?"

"Yeah, you did. You know, if you were interested, I could tutor you. I was a cook in the army for a few years. And now, I do a lot of cooking for the guys at the firehouse. It's one of the unsung duties of being a full-time firefighter, that and cleaning the fire truck. I'm a pretty good cook, if I say so myself. At least, the guys don't complain too much."

This was good. He was just offering her some help. It had nothing to do with the fact that he wanted to strip her down and eat pancakes off her belly or anything. Yeah, sure it didn't.

She perked up a little. "You cooked in the army? How many people did you generally serve at a sitting?"

"Couple a hundred."

"Really? How did you do it? Cook for such a large group, I mean."

Who would have thought the subject of army grub, of all things, would be the key to prying her out of her shell. Most people thought pulling kitchen duty in the military was a punishment, but Alexis was really impressed.

Scott shrugged and tried to live up to her sudden hero worship of his cooking abilities. "I guess you try to keep the menu limited and simple. Do all of the prep work ahead of time. Have as much cooked in advance as you can get away with, you know, the stuff that won't get ruined if it's reheated. And the biggest thing, make sure you have enough or the crowd tends to get hostile."

Alexis had actually whipped out a pen and was jotting down notes on the paper napkin beneath her mug of decaf coffee. Scott put a hand over hers. "I'm serious. If you need help, I'm available."

Very, very available…

She looked up at him, hesitated and then treated him to a gorgeous crooked little smile. "When can you start?"

Chapter 4

Lexi pulled her baseball cap lower on her forehead. This was crazy. Insane. Certifiable. But that thought still didn't stop her as she forged boldly onward, toward the firehouse for her seven a.m. cooking class with Scott the hot fireman. Today's lesson—omelets for twelve. Crazy!

Someone was bound to recognize her. She was surprised Scott hadn't last night. Maybe it was the fact she'd been crying and wasn't wearing any makeup. Or maybe she just wasn't as famous as she thought she was. Whatever. If it meant quitting classes with Chef Frederick, spawn of the devil, and being able to learn how to cook from a man who made her heart flutter every time she looked at him, she was willing to take the chance.

Ladder Company 3. She read the brass plaque on the exterior brick wall of the firehouse. That name seemed really familiar to her for some reason. Hmm. Oh, well. It would come to her eventually. Maybe she'd seen it on the news or something.

Lexi hesitantly opened the door to the firehouse and was greeted by the smell of bacon frying. Steeled by the aroma, and now sure she was not only in the right place but that Scott the cooking fireman and his four pounds of bacon were on the premises, she bravely went all the way in and let the door swing shut behind her.

She followed her nose up the stairs to the kitchen where a large and obviously well used six-burner professional stove dominated the room. Well, actually, the large fireman doing the cooking dominated the space more. She could only see the back of his wavy dark hair as he deftly flipped the bacon, four strips at a time, using a large stainless steel pair of tongs.

The rear view of the tight navy blue pants and t-shirt was nice, but she decided to announce her presence before she started to drool. "Um, hi."

He turned and smiled at her, ice-blue eyes twinkling.

"Morning! I'm surprised to see you."

"I'm sorry. I thought you were serious when you offered…I can go." She edged toward the door.

One hand shot out and grabbed her arm before she got any further. "I *was* serious and I am very happy to see you here. I'm just surprised. You got what, five hours of sleep, maybe six?"

She shrugged. "I don't sleep so well these days. It's just easier to get up and make coffee than lay there awake."

He watched her closely, but didn't ask any questions, just motioned her over to the counter. "Come closer, you're just in time to help prep the omelets."

After he shoved the oversized sheet pan of bacon back into the oven, he steered her to a large cutting board.

"I already cracked all of the eggs into that big steel bowl over there and beat them with a bit of salt and pepper and just a dash of water. For the other ingredients, I bought the cheese pre-shredded and the mushrooms pre-sliced. That saves a lot of work. Now we have to cut the rest of the fresh ingredients."

He placed a green pepper and a really large and extremely sharp looking knife on the wooden board in front of her. She stared at it, and then back up at him.

When she hesitated, he asked, "Do you know how to cut a pepper?"

"Um, with the knife I assume." God, she really was a fraud. On the cooking show everything she needed just magically appeared already prepared in tiny little labeled bowls. Cooking for dummies, only the dummy was the supposed expert.

"I'll show you the first one, then you do the next. Okay?"

She nodded and watched as he deftly deseeded the pepper and diced it into tiny uniform squares. She'd always wondered how the chef at the television studio cut the ingredients so evenly. Scott made it look easy. She hoped it actually was because much too soon, it was her turn and the giant knife, worthy of a horror movie, was now in her hand. Taking a deep breath, she made one slice and then another.

She managed to not cut her fingers off, but the results of her efforts were nowhere near as pretty as his. Big, small, square, oblong, her pepper pieces were everything except uniform.

Lexi sighed. "I'm sorry." It would have been at this point that Chef Frederick would have thrown it all in the garbage, if not actually at her, and made her start again. She glanced nervously up at Scott's face.

He was smiling. "Don't be sorry. You did fine. It just takes practice. Here, let me show you."

He took the weapon-sized knife from her, rocked it back and forth across the pieces a few times until they were all smaller and fairly even, and then scooped it all into a bowl. "There, all fixed. Nothing to worry about. Next, onions."

He made short work of his onion. She struggled a bit with her own, but the onion aroma caused the only tears during the lesson. It was an immeasurable improvement over cooking with the devil—uh, Frederick, where she cried every lesson.

Scott had the patience of a saint with only one rule—she was to never apologize to him for doing something wrong again. Once she got over the constant urge to do just that, she actually started to enjoy herself.

They chopped ham and tomatoes and then they were done with the sharp blade portion of the program.

"Now, this next part might be a little tricky. I can handle four frying pans going at a time, but you may want to work up to that."

She liked a man who could multi-task and was good with his hands, she thought as Scott sprinkled a handful of vegetables and ham into each pan, along with an overly generous-looking ladle of melted butter.

Lexi cringed. "Is all of that butter necessary?"

"If you want to get the omelet out of the pan in one piece, yeah, it is."

Lexi would be a blimp with all this bacon and butter in her own daily diet, but she kept that criticism to herself as she watched him manning each of the four frying pans in turn. It seemed like a lot of unnecessary work. "Um, how come you can't just make one giant omelet and cut it up."

"Because then that wouldn't be an omelet, now would it? Besides, some of the guys don't like onions and mushrooms, so I make half without."

"Oh..." She bit her tongue before the word *sorry* slipped out. Great. Now she felt like a lazy idiot for suggesting what she had thought was a pretty good, time saving idea. She had to give him credit, though, if he did think she was lazy and/or an idiot for her last suggestion, he hid it well.

Since he was continuing on with the lesson without her, she brought her attention back to the frying pans on the burners as he poured a ladle full of egg into each one of the pans. He let things cook a bit and then lifted the firm edges with a rubber spatula so the loose egg mixture slid beneath the cooked. "See what I'm doing here?"

She nodded and tried to watch closer in case there was a trick she was missing or a test later.

"Come here."

Her eyes opened wide. If it had been Chef Frederick, a summons like that would have made her fear for her life. But this was Scott, so instead it caused more than a bit of excitement.

He placed her between him and stove and she felt the heat of his body behind her as strongly as the heat of the stove in front of her. "Watch me first. Loosen the edges, make sure it slips around freely in the pan and then...flip."

The yellow egg discus did an acrobatic flip and landed uncooked side down in the pan. He moved to the next pan, repeating the process. "Wanna try one?"

"No."

He laughed. "Come on. I'll help you. Grab hold of the handle." She did, then his hand covered hers and she swallowed hard. "Loosen the edges with the spatula, slide it around and flip."

She watched the egg pirouette and land perfectly in the pan. "Wow."

"Next one is all yours." He took a step back.

"What if I mess it up?"

"We cover it up with cheese and no one will know."

Lexi took a deep breath, loosened the eggs, made sure they slid around and then she flipped the omelet. It rose in the air in what appeared to her slow motion until it finally came to rest, a bit lopsided, but safe. Given that the egg stayed mostly in the pan and landed on the correct side, she was more than happy, she was ecstatic.

There was definitely a stupid looking grin on her face when she spun around to find Scott smiling back at her. "See! You did great, but there's no time now to gloat about it. We have to get them off the heat before they overcook. Watch me. Shredded cheese on half of each omelet, fold it over, then slide it on to the sheet pan I have waiting. These four go in the oven to keep warm while we make the rest."

Scott was about to start the entire process all over again when a deafening noise filled the firehouse.

Lexi covered her ears before they ruptured. "What is that?" she yelled.

"Fire," he shouted back over the din. Scott quickly shut off all four burners and the oven. "Shit, I gotta go. I'm sorry." He was grabbing all the ingredients off the counter and shoving them into the fridge as he spoke.

She touched his arm to get his attention. "I'll put the stuff in the fridge for you. You go save some lives."

"Thanks." He was half out the door when he looked back. "Another lesson soon?"

She smiled and nodded. As if he could keep her away.

Chapter 5

"Getting a call before breakfast sucks. I could smell the bacon as we were driving away." Troy sat next to Scott in the fire truck complaining.

"Hey, at least it was a false alarm or we'd still be at the call now." That from Antonio, the eternal optimist.

As the driver pulled the truck up to the open garage bay of the firehouse, Scott had to admit, he was hungry himself. "Don't worry, boys. Give me ten minutes and it's omelets and bacon for everyone."

Or maybe not. Scott looked up at the second story of the firehouse and saw smoke billowing out of the kitchen window.

Troy followed his gaze. "What the hell?"

"Holy shit! Did you leave the stove on?" Antonio asked.

"No, of course not." But he had left an unsupervised, unauthorized woman who didn't know how to cook.

Scott leapt out of the truck before it was even parked. He barreled up the stairs to the kitchen, the rest of the crew behind him and skidded to a stop in the doorway.

Alexis stood there, fire extinguisher in her hand and quite a mess of eggs and extinguisher foam on the stove. She turned toward them and her face crumbled. "I'm so sorry."

She looked like she wanted to flee, but since a mass of hungry firemen blocked the only door she just stood there like a deer in headlights.

"Who does she belong to?" Antonio asked from beside him.

No way around it. Scott had to fess up. "Um, that would be me."

Antonio raised a brow and looked with interest from Alexis, back to Scott. "Really?"

That was followed by Troy asking the question that must be on everyone's mind. "Does this mean there's no breakfast?"

And that's when Alexis started to cry.

23

Oh, boy. Scott stepped forward and took the large fire extinguisher canister out of her hands and put it on the floor in the corner, about to tell her it was all right when she blurted out a tearful explanation.

"I thought I could finish making the omelets for you. I made eight more, just like you showed me except one at a time. There was some egg left over and I didn't think it would keep so I was making a thirteenth one, but I must have put too much butter in the pan because when I flipped it, it splashed and the stove went on fire and there was all this smoke and flames shooting in the air..." She looked up at him from under the brim of her baseball cap with a tear-streaked face.

Scott opened the oven and sure enough, there was the pan, filled with omelets. Some were thinner, others fatter, a few a little browner, and one was broken in the middle, but all in all, they didn't look too bad.

"I'll take care of getting this on the table, Scotty. Since you've got your hands full here." Troy tilted his head toward Alexis with a smirk and then grabbed two potholders from the hook on the wall. "Everybody to the table. Bacon and eggs on the way."

Scott was more than happy when the crowd followed Troy and the food to the dining table, leaving him alone with her in the kitchen.

He stepped closer to Alexis, hoping to convince her it was really all right, when she blurted out again that she was sorry, dodged around him and took off through the door.

He followed her down the stairs, barely getting hold of her arm before she got out to the street. Damn, she was fast for a little thing. "Wait. This is nothing to be upset about."

"Nothing to be upset about?" She finally stopped and spun to look up at him. "I almost burnt down your firehouse!"

He stifled a smile. That was pretty ironic, a fire in the firehouse. "But you didn't. You were smart enough to use the fire extinguisher and put it out."

She shook her head and plopped herself down on the stairs, scowling. "I obviously make a better firefighter than a cook."

He smiled. "We're always looking for new recruits." As if that wouldn't be too distracting. Alexis there next to him every day, and in the next bunk at night...

She rolled her eyes at his suggestion.

"Seriously, Alexis. The omelets you made looked great. You did that all on your own with no one there to help you. I'm very proud of you." He lifted her chin and forced her to look at him and at least got the smallest hint of a smile from her. "So what do you want to learn for your next lesson?"

"You're still willing to teach me after this?"

Oh, there was plenty he'd like to teach her, and only some of it involved cooking. "Of course. I told you, I don't frighten easily."

She hesitated. "I would like to learn how to make some hors d'oeuvres and appetizer-type things. Can you do that?"

The demand for hors d'oeuvres was not so big in the army or at the firehouse, but no need for her to know that. He smiled. "Of course I can! I'm the appetizer king. I'm off tonight. Your place or mine?"

He tried to control his smile as she agreed and jotted down her address. Yeah, baby! Alexis' apartment, tonight!

Plans made, Scott watched Alexis drive away then ran up the stairs two at a time, her address clutched in his hand. He blew into the dining room. "Anyone got a cookbook?"

"Looks like you've done enough cooking already this morning judging by the smoke and the smokin' hot girl in the kitchen," one of the guys joked from the end of the table. "Good thing the chief wasn't here. You know the rule about overnight female guests."

Scott rolled his eyes. "She wasn't an overnight guest, just an early morning visitor."

"Sure she was," another guy nodded. "I believe you, Scotty." Laughter and more comments followed from the group.

Here it came, the inevitable teasing. Scott knew he couldn't get away with having a girl in the firehouse, particularly one who'd almost burnt it down, without some ribbing. "Ha, ha. Okay everybody, get all your jabs in now because I have to come up with some recipes for hors d'oeuvres by tonight."

"Hors d'oeuvres! What the hell for?" Troy looked up between bites of omelet.

"Because I'm giving a cooking lesson to the girl you just met at her apartment tonight."

Troy laughed. "Well if this is how she cooks all the time, make sure she's got smoke detectors with fresh batteries installed while you're over there." Still chewing and with his coffee mug in one fist, Troy got up out of his chair, walked toward the kitchen and returned with a book in his hand. He dumped it on the table in front of Scott. "There you go, Scotty. Gift from my sister two years ago. By the way, your girl's omelets are pretty good."

His girl. Hopefully, by tonight she would be. Scott glanced down at the book, which had obviously never even had its colorful and slightly dusty grease-coated cover cracked open in the two years it had sat in the firehouse kitchen. "*Lexi Cooper Cooks.* Never heard of her." Scott started to flip through the pages.

"Sure you have. She's the party planner working with the children's hospital on the bachelor auction fundraiser." Antonio snagged another piece of bacon off the tray.

"She's the one? So it's her fault I'll be parading around half naked and getting auctioned off. Great. Can't wait to meet her at her little pre-auction bachelor mixer cocktail party thing and tell her what I think about her ideas," Troy grumbled.

Scott laughed, but had to be impressed. Judging by the photos, there were some pretty good-looking appetizers in the book. Nothing he couldn't handle making. "Can I borrow this?"

Troy waved a hand absently. "Be my guest. What's mine

is yours, man."

"Hey, Troy. That include your girl Amy?" someone at the other end of the table suggested as Scott shook his head at the bawdy implication, grabbed the last omelet and a few pieces of bacon, and settled in with the cookbook to make plans for his evening with Alexis.

Hopefully he'd work up to a dessert lesson next, maybe something involving whipped cream. His mind reeled with the possibilities as he flipped the book over to look in the index in the back...and stopped dead.

There, smiling up at him from the back cover of the book, holding a whisk in one hand and a bowl in the other was his cooking student Alexis; only she was really Lexi Cooper, famous cookbook author.

"Scotty. What's wrong, man? You look like you've seen a ghost," Antonio asked from across the table.

Scott swallowed, flipped the book back over to hide the picture and forced a smile. "Nothing. Just can't believe I have to actually teach how to make hors d'oeuvres, that's all."

And that was the question of the day—of the whole damn year—why the hell was he teaching Lexi Cooper how to cook?

~

Lexi's doorbell rang at barely five-fifteen. Jeez. Scott only got off his shift at five. What did he do, race over? Maybe he was just anxious to see her. She was sure anxious to see him. She definitely approved of his hands-on cooking techniques and had to admit in spite of the small fire, which she had put out she reminded herself, she really had the hang of making omelets now. She'd even tried making one at home all on her own, and was able to actually eat it. That was a step in the right direction.

Of course, she'd had to break the brand new omelet pan that one of the cookware companies had sent her as a promotional gift out of its box first. But the eggs tasted great and then she'd written an article about how to cook brunch for a crowd for her weekly lifestyle column. She'd thrown in a few tidbits about table linens and centerpieces and *viola*, she'd gone from firehouse to foo-foo in one swipe of her pen, or computer keyboard as it were. It had been a very productive day.

And now she was about to have an evening all alone with Scott. Lexi flung open the door, excited to get right down to more lessons...and maybe a little something else, too.

"Something you want to tell me?" Scott, still in his blue uniform pants and t-shirt, braced himself against the doorframe with one hand and held her cookbook in the other. Her own photo stared back at her from the back cover, smiling. Uh, oh.

She swallowed hard as her heart sank and she took a step back. "You better come inside. This may take awhile to explain."

Scott raised a brow. "Ya think?"

That figured. She finally found a guy she liked that by some miracle seemed to like her back, and she was even actually learning how to cook, and now it was all a big mess.

This is all Robert's fault!

"Who the hell is Robert? You got a husband, too, on top of a best selling cookbook?"

Had she said that out loud? "No. Robert is my agent."

He looked relieved at that revelation. Or maybe she just wanted him to look relieved at the fact she was single.

Actually, he wasn't as angry as he could have been over the fact that she'd lied to him about who she was. He stood there, though, looking as if he wanted her to give him a good explanation. Good or not, the only thing she had to give was the truth.

Now that her hand was forced, she almost felt relieved. No more hiding. No more lying. Of course, it meant her career might be over. She swallowed hard at that thought.

"Sit down." She poured them both a glass of wine with a less than steady hand and sat down in a chair opposite where

Scott sat on the couch. The delicate stemmed wine glass looked ridiculous in his big hands. "Sorry I don't have any beer to offer you."

He laughed. "Oh, believe me. Rubbing alcohol would be good enough right now. This is fine. This...and an explanation."

She nodded, took a swallow and then a deep breath, letting it out slowly. "Okay. It all started about three years ago..."

She told him about everything. Her evil boss and the blowout when she quit the PR firm. Her life-long desire to be a writer. The opportunity at the local paper for a weekly lifestyle column, her agent Robert and the little white lie that had snowballed, leading to the cookbook offer, the television show and even more lies. She told him about Chef Frederick and the soufflés he'd thrown at her. And finally, she threw in the fact that if she didn't learn to cook in two weeks, there would be no food at the hundred-dollar a head pre-bachelor auction fundraiser that the entire board of the children's hospital would be attending with their high power guests.

"So that's it." She concluded with a sigh and realized that this was the first time she'd breathed freely in weeks. No wonder she was crying over eggs lately, the stress had been overwhelming. "You know what? It feels really good to have that all off my chest. Although I am going to be publicly ruined and humiliated and my career will be over. Maybe I will have to become a firewoman."

Scott put his now empty wine glass on the table, rose and knelt in front of her chair. He took her hands in his large warm ones and squeezed.

God, he was so sweet, even now, and she felt even worse for deceiving him. "I am so sorry I didn't tell you the truth. Do you think you can forgive me?"

He nodded. "I already have. And your career isn't over. I won't tell a soul about your secret."

"Really? But what about the other guys from the kitchen this morning?"

Scott shook his head. "First of all, firefighters are a family and we stick together. No one will say a thing if I ask them not to. And FYI, no one else recognized you this morning, but they will eventually figure it out since you're going to be hanging around with me a lot."

Her spirits soared. He wanted her around him, *a lot*. "I am?"

"Yeah, you are because I have an idea. I am going to help you save your fundraiser and your career."

Her heart skipped a beat. "Why would you do that?"

He laughed. "Well, one reason is because I'm in that calendar and it will be really embarrassing if the fundraiser is a flop."

Lexi's mouth fell open. No wonder Ladder 3 was so familiar to her. She pulled her hands away from his and jumped up out of her chair, nearly toppling him on his butt.

She located her copy of the Hunky Firemen calendar buried under a pile of papers on her desk and looked at the cover shot with amazement. There, standing in front of the firehouse she'd nearly burnt down just hours before, were a dozen shirtless, muscled firemen, including Scott and some guys she recognized as being the ones so worried about breakfast being ruined this morning.

Lexi flipped through the pages and finally came face to face with Scott, Mr. July, is all his glory. A shadow fell across the page, he was next to her in the flesh now. He groaned. "It's even more embarrassing than I imagined. Can we put that away and talk about my plan?"

She turned to smile at him as he looked suddenly shy. "Sure." She'd have plenty of time later to gaze at him when she was alone. Was it inappropriate to hang a calendar next to the bed?

He pulled her over to the couch. "So, I'm thinking that since this is a firehouse fundraiser, and since firefighters are known for being good cooks, you could have all the cooking for the event done by actual firemen."

She looked at him in shock. "That is a brilliant idea! But

will they do it? Will they help me?"

"Of course they will, once I ask them. We'll go through your cookbook and choose some menu ideas. You have actually read your own cookbook, haven't you?" He smirked.

"Yes, but we're hoping to sell five hundred tickets to this event. That's a lot of hors d'oeuvres."

"So? First of all, we can buy a lot of the stuff prepared. As for the rest, we've got four firehouses represented in that calendar, there are plenty of hands to do the last minute prep work and four kitchens to prepare it in. And really, only the guys from my house will know you can't cook. All the rest will think having firemen cater the party is just another gimmick to sell tickets."

"You'd lie to all those other firefighters for me?"

Scott gazed at her for a second, hesitating. She was asking a great deal of him. Could she really expect him to deceive his brother firefighters?

"Outright lie, no, but I won't have to. I'm going to coach you and you are going to learn to cook, so by the fundraiser there will be no need to lie, only to bend the truth a little bit."

Or a lot, she added silently, but appreciated his offer. "You are so sweet."

He laughed. "Not that sweet. I'm serious about you learning to cook everything we serve at that party. I mean everything. Even if we end up buying five hundred appetizer-sized quiches frozen and just bake and serve them for the party, you are still going to learn how to make quiche from scratch. That's the only way I'll do this. Got it?"

"Yes." Lexi leaned forward and brushed her lips lightly across his. "And thanks. You saved my life."

He cleared his throat. "That's my job." Was he blushing?

"No, this is definitely not part of your job. How can I ever thank you."

"No need to thank me." He leaned back and breathed in

deeply. "Let's get a pad of paper and that cookbook and start planning."

Chapter 6

"Deeper, from the belly. Like this. Ho, ho, ho!"

Someone needed to tell this guy that although he looked like Santa Claus, belly that shook like a bowl full of jelly and all, he was not actually St. Nick himself.

Delusions of Santa or not, Scott attempted his best imitation of the teacher's ho, ho, ho-ing anyway. If he was going to have to play Santa the week before the bachelor auction to promote the calendar and event, he better learn how to do it now, during the special crash course set up for the firemen at Santa School. He ho'd, the teacher listened, nodded and luckily for him, his ho's were sufficient, because the teacher left him and moved on to the next victim.

When the coast was clear, Scott leaned over to Antonio and Troy. "So are you guys in? Will you help me and Lexi cook for the event?"

Troy scowled. "It would serve her right for coming up with this humiliating auction and event if we didn't help."

"Come on, Troy. If five hundred people are actually willing to pay a hundred dollars each just to spend a few hours mingling with us at a private cocktail party before the public auction, we have to do it. Think of all that money for the hospital if they actually sell all those tickets. It was a smart idea. Lexi Cooper knows her stuff, even if she can't cook," Antonio whispered.

"Remember, no one outside of our house can know she can't cook. If the press gets a hold of that, she'll be ruined," Scott hissed.

"I know, I know. So now I have to be groped at a party, auctioned off half naked *and* help you and her cook hors d'oeuvres for five hundred. I'm really glad you met this Lexi person, Scotty. Have I mentioned that to you before?" Troy asked sarcastically as the teacher spun around with a giant "SHHH!"

Scott suppressed a smile as Troy cocked a brow that said 'thanks a lot' in his direction. Yup, they were all just like brothers.

Apparently the Ho-ing lesson was over and the teacher approached the blackboard and wrote in dusty yellow chalk *How to Handle a Crying Child…*

Scott dutifully picked up his pen. He fully intended on taking notes, but somehow, his mind wasn't on board with that idea and he began to daydream—extremely vivid and tantalizing daydreams.

In his mind's eye, he was wearing a Santa suit and was seated in the big gold throne set up in Bryant's Department Store's holiday department. Lexi was there, too, dressed as the sexiest elf he'd ever seen. She sauntered over to him in a very short red velvet skirt and high-heeled black boots. He could feel the white fur cuffs on the sleeves of her low-cut top brush his face as she wrapped her arms around his neck and crawled into his lap. His hands cupped her shapely and surprisingly bare ass.

"Naughty elf! You're not wearing any underwear!" he'd say. Then Lexi would say, "No, Santa, I'm not. What will you do to punish me? Are you going to spank me with those big hands of yours?"

"Maybe if you show me how nice you can be, my sexy elf, I'll give you a big candy cane instead."

The fantasy got even more interesting as Scott pulled his chair up closer beneath the shelter of the desk and enjoyed the triple X movie running in his head.

At the end of class, Scott glanced down at his blank pad of paper and noticed he didn't have a single word written, not one note on how to deal with crying children. Oh well, he didn't know how to deal with crying women, either, may as well be consistent.

What Scott did have after the class, however, was an overwhelming desire to drive over to see Lexi—more than just 'see' her actually—and a shift starting at the firehouse in less than half an hour.

He sighed. Even if he and Lexi were up to that much anticipated physical stage in their relationship, which they weren't, there wouldn't have been time. Half an hour including travel time…not even Santa himself could pull that feat off, magic sleigh, reindeer and all.

Besides, Scott had frozen up the other night when Lexi had done nothing more than given him a chaste little thank-you kiss for offering to help her cook for the event. He wanted her on her back and naked so badly, he hadn't dared to return her kiss only to find out she didn't want him in the same way.

He'd been with Linda for too long. He'd forgotten the hellish insecurity that came along with starting a new relationship. The dance a man must do to determine if any advance he made would be welcomed or met with a slap or worse, the I-only-like-you-as-a-friend speech. He had to find out where he stood with her, and soon, or he might explode.

Were he writing to the North Pole, Scott's only request of Santa this year would be that he awaken Christmas morning with Lexi as his present, wrapped in nothing but his bed sheets. And if that image didn't inspire a belly full of heartfelt ho, ho, ho's, he didn't know what would!

Just the possibility of having more with Lexi was definitely worth the trouble as well as the fear. Hell, just the promise of Lexi had him and his entire house cooking for five hundred people! But how could he not help her, the poor thing was so nervous about this gig.

If it weren't for this event of hers, he would have sucked up his own fears and already put on the charm, full steam ahead. She liked him. He was sure of that. Now, he would just have to make sure she *really* liked him in a let's-get-naked kind of way without making a fool of himself. And he'd set himself single-mindedly to that task the moment this fundraiser was over, if the frustration didn't kill him first.

Oh well. Good things come to those who wait, or something like that. They had less than two weeks to pull off the fundraising event of the year. He'd waited this long to meet her, he'd just have to wait a little longer to get to the rest. With that agonizing thought in mind, he headed for a

Trilogy No. 106: Nice & Naughty

very long twenty-four hour shift at the firehouse.

Chapter 7

Lexi stood in the television studio, hands on her hips, scowl firmly in place. "I want to start doing my own prep and cooking on the show!"

Robert grabbed her arm and dragged her into the corner of the studio. "No. You aren't ready yet."

Her eyes opened wide. She didn't believe what she was hearing. "You are the one who encouraged me to..." she spotted a workman nearby and lowered her voice to a bare hiss, "...learn to cook in the first place."

Robert nodded. "Yes I did, and I am very proud of you, but you are not ready. Not yet. And stop frowning at me, you'll get wrinkles."

Lexi hated when he treated her like a child and hated even more when he was right. She tried to smooth the frown from her brow. But she still felt she was right about the cooking thing. In the last week, she'd squeezed in as many cooking lessons with Scott as both of their schedules would allow.

She'd successfully learned to create almost everything on the menu for the fundraising event. With Scott's tutelage she'd made spinach-stuffed pastry triangles, sesame chicken skewers, Swedish meatballs, tiny lamb chops, stuffed mushroom caps, crab cakes and a few other things that escaped her at the moment.

She was sure she was ready to cook on the show. "Can I at least cut my own damn vegetables on camera?"

"I don't know, can you?" At Robert's condescending tone, Lexi had visions of her grade school teacher who loved that very question to illustrate her 'may I' vs. 'can I' grammar lesson whenever a student asked incorrectly.

"Yeeessss, I can. So may I?"

Dammit! It was her show. She shouldn't have to ask permission to do squat. If she wanted to cook naked while standing on her head they should all agree whole-heartedly. She was the expert, after all.

Then she remembered what she sometimes managed to forget when the lights and cameras were on. She didn't know squat about cooking and Robert, who was always looking out for her, knew that all too well. "Please, Robert? I think I'm ready for at least chopping vegetables. I've been practicing."

He softened visibly with her begging. "You are making tomato sauce with macerated basil leaves on the show today. Can you do that?"

"Sure I can...as soon as you tell me what macerated means."

Robert raised a brow. "It means to cut the basil leaves into extremely thin strips...look, I don't think this is the day for your chopping debut."

"Yes it is. Show me the macerated basil the studio prepared and I'll copy it on camera." *Macerated*. What a horrible word. It sounded too much like *emaciated* for her taste. What insane chef came up with *that* unappealing cooking term? She had a sudden vision of crazy Chef Frederick and immediately rescinded her question.

With a big sigh, Robert led her to the kitchen on set where she attempted to unobtrusively dissect the shredded basil while trying to figure out how to recreate it herself. She wished Scott were here, for many reasons, only one of which being he could show her how to do this. Of course, smelling his warm scent and feeling his strong hands show her how to hold the knife wouldn't be unwelcome either. If only he'd make his move and put those hands on her...

"Lexi. Please save this display of bravado and independence for a later show." Now it was Robert who was begging and using that tone again, the one that made her feel like a child.

"Nope. I got it. No problem. Let's start filming. I'm fine."

Lexi watched Robert shaking his head as he walked away and had a sudden memory of her father often looking the exact same way. Oh, well. At least she was consistent when it came to frustrating the men in her life.

The director yelled for quiet, the lights flashed on brightly and the cameras swung towards her. Lexi read the prompter like the pro she supposedly was and whizzed through the steps for the recipe. She breezed through the heating of the pan, the addition of the oil, the browning of the chopped garlic (she'd learned how to operate the garlic press last lesson with Scott so she demonstrated that easily) and she had just added the canned tomatoes when it came time to talk about the dreaded macerated basil.

Having mentally made a plan of attack before the cameras started to roll, she stacked the basil leaves, one on top of another until there was a tall pile in front of her and then took the large knife in her hand. She breathed in deeply and plunged right in, making long thin slices out of the basil, only to realize that she had to also read the teleprompter at the same time. She hadn't taken that into consideration during the planning phase.

You can do this, she told herself and raised her eyes to the teleprompter while still slicing…and immediately felt the sting as the knife sliced into her flesh as well as the basil. She stifled a yelp and continued to smile for the camera, grabbed a kitchen towel to hide her hand and improvised. "There, you get the idea. Let's just skip ahead and add the basil I prepared before the show to the tomato mixture…"

"Cut!"

Cut. Yup, that is what she'd done to herself, all right. She let her on-camera smile disappear and dared to glance down at the now red kitchen towel still in her hand.

"Jesus, Lexi! You're bleeding." The director and half the crew suddenly surrounded her.

"I'm fine." Of course, she hadn't dared to actually look yet.

Robert pushed his way through the group to stand beside her. "Give her some space. Lexi, let me see."

Not so upset about his treating her like a child any longer, Lexi thrust her hand at Robert and looked the other way, afraid of what she might see. At least she hadn't noticed any fingertips on the cutting board. Surely, that was a good sign, although the amount of blood soaking the towel was not.

"It's not that deep, but you probably should go to the emergency room anyway. It might require a stitch or two."

Stitches! She'd never needed stitches in her life. "No, really. I don't think I need stitches. Can't we just bandage it up and I'll finish the show?"

There was that frustrated sigh again. "*If* I can get it to stop bleeding, you can finish the show. Then I'm taking you to a doctor to at least have it properly cleaned and looked at. Got it?"

She nodded as Robert called out over his shoulder, "Can somebody bring me a first aid kit, please?"

He couldn't hide the 'I told you so' expression he wore on his face, but he didn't say it out loud. Lexi didn't need him to say it; her own bloody finger was enough of a reminder.

Chapter 8

Scott stood at Lexi's door and rang the bell, as ready as he'd ever be to withstand the temptation of being near her again in the flesh. Given the fact that he thought of her every waking moment when they were apart and thought about stripping her naked the entire time they were together, he was living in a constant state of aroused frustration.

Being with her for their lessons and having to act professional and as if he didn't want to roll around with her on the kitchen floor was unbearable. But being on shift at the firehouse was also killing him. All that time to sit around and think about her. He'd actually found himself wishing for a fire so he'd have something to take his mind off of this torture.

Realizing what a sad state he was in, he'd made sure he'd taken care of his own physical gratification privately before coming to see Lexi tonight. Since he got a hard-on just thinking about her nowadays, he knew there was no way he could be in the same room with her and not have his body react to her. Smelling the now familiar scent of her citrus shampoo mingled with that of whatever food they were making. Watching her chest rise and fall as she breathed. Seeing her bite her lower lip while she concentrated...

He'd finally just taken matters into his own hands, so to speak. Now, there would be no sexual distraction. He was prepared for the next cooking class—tiny quiche appetizers.

Lexi had gone to the store and bought all the ingredients for the lesson today while he was working. Everything should be good to go.

Or so he thought...until she opened the door looking like any man's wet dream. Her face was flushed and the redness ran all the way down to her exposed cleavage. The short, achingly tight bicycle pants she was wearing didn't help much either.

"Hi. Come on in, but you're going to want to take off your jacket, probably your shirt too. There's something wrong with the heat in the building. It's like ninety degrees in here even with the windows open. I can't imagine how hot it's going to get once we turn the oven on."

Oh, Scott could imagine how hot things were going to get, all right. He stripped off his jacket and sweatshirt but chose to suck it up and keep his t-shirt on. He was a fireman, he could handle extreme temperatures. It was the extremely hot girl in front of him, the one with the shapely behind leading him to the kitchen, that he was having trouble not getting scorched by.

"I went to the store and bought the stuff. I even tried making a batch of pie crust on my own for the quiches, but it's so sticky, no matter how much flour I add."

He dragged his gaze away from the flour stain on her tank top—it was located just over her left boob—and tried to process what she was saying. Oh, yeah. Flour. Piecrusts. "It's too hot. You can't work with dough when it's this hot. The dough has to be cold."

She sighed. "Then what are we going to do?"

He wrestled his mind away from the image of what he'd like to do and went to squat near the closest radiator. The heat pumping steadily out of it was nearly as unbearable as his urge to strip them both naked until they were sweaty for quite a different reason. "Put the dough in the fridge for now. I'll take care of the heat until your landlord fixes whatever is wrong. You got a screwdriver?"

She nodded. "The kind with the tip shaped like an X or the kind without?" She actually made an X shape with her two fingers when she asked him that question.

He smiled. As well as being cooking challenged, Lexi apparently wasn't mechanically inclined either. "A straight screwdriver is fine." He decided he better elaborate. "The kind without the X."

Once in possession of the tool, he turned off the radiator in the kitchen. "That should help, but we'll have to wait for it to cool down in here before we work on the pie crust."

"Could you turn off the radiator in the bedroom, too? I'll

42

never be able to sleep tonight if it's this hot in there."

He swallowed, picturing her sweaty and naked, tossing and turning in bed, unable to sleep. "The bedroom? Um, sure."

"Great. I'll show you where it is." She walked ahead of him as his internal warning sensor screamed at him. Danger! Danger, Scott O'Malley!

As he crouched between the bed and the radiator, it didn't help one bit when she plopped herself down on the mattress with a bounce. His eyes went directly to her bouncing breasts, like a compass to true north, as the screwdriver slipped and rammed into his palm. At least the pain of the sharp tool jabbing into his hand brought his mind back up from the dark depths to which it had sunk.

"Damn."

"You hurt yourself. Let me see."

"Nope. I'm fine. Nothing to see." Scott shook his head vehemently, ignoring the small crimson puddle forming in his palm. If she started tending his wounds, he knew his resolve would be lost and he wouldn't be able to keep his hands off of her any longer.

"You are not fine. You're bleeding!" Lexi grabbed a tissue from the bedside table and kneeling next to him, pressed it into his hands.

He looked down at her small hand in his, then up to her face, level with him as they both knelt. "Thanks."

Oh, boy. As predicted, the close confines and her concern for him were definitely not helping. He grasped for any distraction, and then he noticed the bandage on her finger. "Hey. What happened to your finger?"

"I tried to skip ahead a few lessons and cut myself trying to macerate basil." She bit her lip, looking embarrassed and adorable, and that was it. He realized he couldn't take any more. With that one little action his resistance was totally gone.

Besides, he rationalized, what could one little kiss hurt? Really, he should be able to handle just that. With that in mind, Scott gave in to the urge. He leaned forward and touched his mouth to hers, drawing her bottom lip between his teeth so he could nibble on it himself.

Her breath caught in her throat and then he was totally lost in her. Both injuries forgotten, his hands slid around her waist and he felt the hot damp skin of her back where her top and shorts didn't quite meet.

He broke away just long enough to say her name before he was kissing her again, forcing them both down onto the carpet. She felt so right beneath him, even if they were on the floor wedged between the wall and the bed.

With every passing moment that she didn't pull away and say she liked him as 'just a friend', he grew more encouraged. But the possibility of her stopping him still hung in the air like an axe above his head.

And then she did it, what he feared most, she drew back and held him off with one hand.

He stifled a groan and pulled away, kneeling over her now, waiting for the inevitable blow off.

"I can't do this like this."

Head hanging, he closed his eyes and nodded.

She continued. "It's too damn hot for all these clothes. I want you naked."

His eyes flew open. "You do?"

Lexi grinned wickedly, running one fingernail tantalizingly down the t-shirt covering his chest. "Mmm, hmm. I've been enjoying my calendar, but there's no substitute for the real thing."

The real thing. He understood that better than she knew. His groin ached with wanting her in spite of the fact he'd jerked off not an hour ago. "Oh, you got that right."

He pulled off his shirt, flung it somewhere and lowered himself onto her again. His tongue pushed between her lips as she raised her hips off the floor to press against him.

His hands roamed up her body with a groan, pushing the hem of her shirt higher. "I want you naked, too," he breathed against her mouth.

She pulled back again. "I want you in that bed."

He couldn't complain about that request. "How about we both get naked and I'll meet you there?"

"You got it."

There was a brief whirlwind of flying clothing as they raced to get to the bed. Lexi, who hadn't had to deal with shoelaces the way Scott did, got there first.

He took a step toward her and stumbled with an "Ow!" Why was there always some kind of obstacle standing between him and this beautiful, willing, and now nude woman?

She giggled. "What did you do to yourself now?"

Bending down, he grabbed the offending object and held it in the air for her to see. "I stepped on the screwdriver."

She laughed. "Put it away in the drawer before you hurt yourself more and can't perform."

"Oh, I'll be able to perform, don't you worry about that." He hobbled to the nightstand, pulled open the drawer and stopped, just staring.

"What's wrong? Oh my god!" Red faced, Lexi suddenly realized what he'd seen and tried to shove the drawer shut, but Scott was far more motivated to keep it open.

"Oh, no, no, no." One hand held the drawer open while the other pulled out a large pink penis-shaped dildo, complete with battery pack. As he grabbed it, his hand must have brushed the 'on' switch because the thing started to gyrate and quiver all on its own. He smiled down at her on the bed. "What do we have here?"

Lexi flung herself onto her stomach and buried her face in the pillow. "I can't believe you found that."

"That's not all I found." He reached into the drawer again and pulled out the fireman calendar…opened to July.

She raised her face just enough to see what he was talking about and then buried it again. "I'm so totally humiliated."

Lexi was naked and face down on the bed. There were far better things he should be doing, but Scott couldn't help himself, he had to ask. "Lexi. Do you actually...you know...to my picture?"

"I'm not going to answer that." The pillow muffled Lexi's voice, but he heard her just fine and knew that a 'no comment' was as good as a yes. Wasn't that interesting. Women did *that*, too.

Still a bit in shock at the discovery that women did the same thing men did, but with toys, he managed to turn off the pink thing, part of it which looked suspiciously like a bunny rabbit, ears and all, and put it back in the drawer without activating it again.

Smiling with satisfaction, Scott crawled into bed and laid the length of his body along Lexi's back, nestling his erection snugly between her legs.

Nuzzling the back of her neck, he whispered, "At least you had a picture. When I do *that* thinking about you, I have to use my imagination."

She slowly turned her head and he saw just the side of her reddened face. "You think about me and...you know?"

He nodded. If she could face the embarrassment of being outed doing that, then he could, too. "Yeah, pretty much every day since the night I met you. You remember, the night of the infamous egg incident." He joked with her but then got perfectly serious. "There's nothing for you to be embarrassed about, believe me."

She bit her lower lip, and yet again, he had the urge to take over and do it for her. He stroked her face with a fingertip and nudged himself a little deeper between her legs.

Her eyelids drifted closed as she breathed in deeply and spread her thighs enough for him to move freely between them. He slowly inched closer to his final destination, thinking that this was far better than any of his fantasies.

Brushing her hair aside, he ran his tongue along her neck and whispered, "You're right, though. There's nothing quite like the real thing."

He pushed just the tip of his erection into her and she sighed. He nudged again and she pushed back against him, driving him deeper within her until he could go no further.

"Oh, god." He closed his eyes at the sensation, hardly believing he was suddenly buried inside the woman he'd only dreamed about, night after night, since he'd first seen her.

He covered both of her hands with his and began an unhurried, leisurely pace, running his lips over her shoulders and neck as he loved her. There was no way he was going to rush something he had waited for so long.

Lexi's head lolled to one side and she sighed, eyes closed. "I could do this all night."

He couldn't imagine anything better.

"I'll do my best," he whispered, then nipped her neck lightly with his teeth. "Of course, if I get tired, there's always Mr. Pink over there in the drawer." He enjoyed watching her turn pink again herself, but he was only partially teasing.

They could definitely do this all night, and he intended on taking advantage of all available props she may have during that time. He wondered what other toys may be hidden around. If she didn't have any others, he knew a store where he could buy some for her for future use. That thought got him even more excited.

He picked up the pace and slipped a hand beneath her, finding the spot he knew would send her over the edge. Being inside Lexi was amazing, but being inside her while she shattered around him would be a dream come true, literally. "God, Lexi. I've wanted this for so long."

Lexi began to shudder. Her breaths came in gasps as her hips angled toward the hand that played between her thighs. "Then what the hell took you so long?" she huffed as her muscles crashed around him.

At the moment, he really couldn't remember why the hell he had waited so long. Whatever the reason, it wasn't good enough to have denied him this with her.

And now that he finally had her, he didn't want it to end, but feeling her orgasm, he realized that no amount of will

47

power would prevent him from following right behind her as she came. Just as nothing would keep him from wanting to do this with her forever.

That realization, that Lexi was *the one*, nearly floored him. It was just like the guys had said. He knew, without a shadow of a doubt. That thought shook him as much as Lexi's climax as wave upon wave continued to rack her with him spent but still inside of her.

By the time Lexi's body calmed, Scott had sunk into a feeling of complete and utter peace. It wouldn't have surprised him one bit to discover he was actually glowing from sex and yeah, love, as they both lay in a panting heap on the bed.

When Scott could move again, he kissed Lexi's head softly and rolled off of her, deciding to keep his recent epiphany about being in love with her to himself for the time being. He had a lot to think about first before he made any confessions.

But in the meantime…

"What the hell does *macerate* mean?" He finally remembered the question he hadn't bothered to ask before, during the heat of passion.

Lexi flipped over, looking excited and unbelievably tempting. "You don't know?"

He shook his head, still craving this woman and not really caring about the answer to the question any longer. Instead, he began seriously considering how he could enjoy a little play with Lexi and Mr. Pink until he recovered enough for another bout.

She, in the meantime, smiled hugely at him. "You mean I know something about cooking that you don't know? So, the student has surpassed the master, would you say?" she suggested, looking smug.

"Looks like," he agreed, mentally making a plan of attack while his hand stroked the side of her bare breast idly.

She kept talking, undeterred. "You know, even though I did cut myself today, I think I'm really getting the hang of it.

And for the first time, I really believe I'm going to be able to pull this fundraising event off."

"I know you will." He knew that for an absolute fact. He did not mention, however, the order he'd placed for frozen hors d'oeuvres for five hundred or the schedule of cooking shifts and menu plans he'd hung in the four firehouses that day. Instead, at least for tonight, he'd let her think she was handling it on her own.

He gauged the distance to the nightstand as she smiled at him. "Thank you for having confidence in me."

"You're welcome." Then he rolled on top of her, kissing her and nipping at her bottom lip lightly with his teeth while reaching for the drawer. He watched with amusement as her eyes opened wide in surprise when she heard the unmistakable sound of the vibrator turning on.

For the rest of the night, Scott made sure there was no more talk of cooking.

The End

MR. DECEMBER

Chapter 1

Jason Bryant knew two things with absolute certainty: 1) retail during the holiday season was absolute insanity, and 2) he wouldn't want it any other way. Although, glancing around the already frazzled faces of the store's employees, he had to wonder if he was the only one who felt that way.

Sheesh! It was only the day after Thanksgiving and they all already looked like they'd been to war and back. He'd seen happier faces in photos taken during the Great Depression.

Meanwhile, Jason couldn't be happier as the post-holiday sale adrenaline rush surged through his body. Black Friday, the day retail institutions went from running in the red to the black often with the highest one-day intake of the year. Just the phrase took his breath away!

He rubbed his hands together and then checked his watch. Six-thirty. He clapped his hands to get the attention of the large group assembled in the break room. "People. We open in half an hour."

There was a collective groan over the extra early opening and the extended holiday hours. He decided to continue his inspirational speech undaunted, hoping his personal contribution of fresh hot coffee and donuts would help to boost morale.

"Come on! You know the song; it's the most wonderful time of the year. Smile. We love our customers and we want them to love us. Get some coffee, meditate, do whatever you have to do but get yourselves merry by the time those doors open in thirty minutes."

It wasn't exactly Shakespeare's Saint Crispin's Day speech from *Henry V*. Hell, it wasn't even the 'win one for the Gipper' speech from that old Ronald Reagan movie, but it would have to do. The employees shuffled at a zombie-like pace toward the coffee as Jason considered getting an inspirational sign to hang above the door of the break room. Something like the sign that hung in the locker room at

Notre Dame to inspire the football team before a game. Something to consider. He'd add it to the already lengthy list of things to do currently entered in his electronic organizer.

It was hard for Jason to even imagine that the seemingly living dead who were his employees didn't share his holiday excitement. Admittedly, he may have different feelings about the day after Thanksgiving than the others in the room. He was sure all they could think about was the leftover turkey waiting in their fridge and the football games they were missing on television. While all Jason could think about was the energy that positively radiated from this old building at Christmas, until the bricks and mortar seemed to possess a life force all their own.

Bryant's Department Store was like a gracious lady bedecked in her gayest finery during the holiday season, and every tourist and local came to admire her. Jason had loved Bryant's at holiday time ever since his Grandpa Bryant first brought him here to sit in Santa's lap. That was before Jason had even learned to walk. Since his grandfather's retirement, the store was now Jason's ship to steer, and he intended on navigating the staid local institution into an even brighter future.

Jason bounced on his toes, as if a giant ball of energy trapped in his body was trying to get out. If only he could send some of his vigor the way of those around him. He was considering some options when his assistant came up and tapped him on the shoulder.

"Peggy! You look festive." She did, dressed in a green pantsuit with a red berry pin. He recognized both items as being store stock and smiled. Peggy was a loyal store employee, he'd wager right down to her Bryant's private label underwear.

The older woman, who had assisted his grandfather for over twenty years and now belonged to him, raised one painted-on eyebrow. "We'll see how festive you feel after I tell you what's happening."

Jason frowned. Whatever it was, he was not going to let

it ruin his first Black Friday at Bryant's helm. He hadn't worked his way up from stockroom clerk, to floor associate, to manager, to Chief Operating Officer to let anything get in his way now. He gripped Peggy with one hand on each of her bony shoulders and stared deeply into her eyes. "What is it, Peggy?"

She released a loud cackle. "Well, Jesus. It isn't that bad. No one's dead. I just got a call from the Santa who's supposed to be here today."

Jason nodded. "Mmm, hmm. One of the local firemen promoting the charity calendar." There was a stack of calendars for sale at every register in the store.

"Yup. Mr. December, Troy O'Donnell, Ladder Company No. 3. Six feet tall and two hundred pounds of solid muscle, from what I can see."

"Yes, Peggy. I get it. What about Mr. O'Donnell?"

"He ain't coming. His wife or girlfriend or somebody called and said he's been throwing up for hours." Peggy waved a dismissive hand, seeming far less interested in Mr. O'Donnell's marital status than she was in his physical attributes. "Not sure if it's the flu or just a stomach bug, but he was up, getting dressed and trying to come here when she called me so I could tell him myself, officially, that he should stay the hell home."

He agreed, but hoped Peggy hadn't actually used the phrase 'stay the hell home'. "Of course he should stay home. It wouldn't do to have Santa vomiting on the children, or spreading a stomach virus to our customers and staff."

"That's what I told him. But now what do we do about getting a Santa last minute?"

"Have you called the firehouse to see if they have a spare?"

Peggy laughed at that. "Have you seen those firemen in that calendar? If they do have a spare, they can send him over to my house!"

Yes, Jason had seen the nearly nude fireman calendar, all twelve months of it. Aside from selling it at his store, Peggy had it hanging in her office for almost a month now even though it didn't officially start until January of next year. The item seemed to be very popular with the ladies. Apparently from her rundown on Mr. December, Peggy had memorized all of the hunky firemen's stats already.

He rolled his eyes and had to smile. Peggy was seventy if she was a day.

"Stop rolling your eyes at me. I'm old, I'm not dead. And yeah, I called. They got nobody for us today. All of their fireman Santas are either on duty at the firehouse or spoken for elsewhere. They got them playing Claus all over town, you know, not just here. The children's hospital, the library. They said they might be able to swing somebody for tomorrow if he's still not better."

Jason pursed his lips as an idea struck him. He'd often wanted to be a fly on the wall in the store, see what his employees were up to when he wasn't around, hear unsolicited comments from customers. But his face was too well known in the store. This little misfortune could turn out to be a perfect opportunity.

"Peggy. We've got the Santa suit here, correct?"

"Yup. Up in my office. Just got it out of the dry cleaners."

"Excellent! I'll arrange for a Santa. Oh, and I'll be out of touch for the day, so if anyone calls for me, just take a message."

Peggy cocked an already sharply arching black brow at him. "What are you up to?"

He winked at her and held one finger up to his lips to indicate she should keep quiet.

She shook her head at him. "You've got the devil in you, just like your grandpa."

Jason smiled and laid an arm around her shoulders, steering them both out of the door of the break room. "And you've worked for us both for over twenty years now. So what does that say about you, my dear Peggy?"

She let out a loud crackling laugh. "It says that I know

I'll have a lot more fun working for a devil than a saint, that's what. Come on. I may have to find more padding for the suit. You're in better shape than last year's guy."

He grinned at her. She knew him too well, the mark of a great assistant.

Santa Claus for a day, this was an unexpected treat! He was feeling jollier by the minute. In fact, in the world of retail, Jason considered himself to be Mr. December. Maybe he should print his own calendar. Hunky men of retail...something for the list.

~

Five hours and what felt like countless hundreds of children later, Jason was reconsidering his initial opinion about the merits of the Santa Claus business. He experienced a veritable rainbow of behaviors when it came to the children, with the emphasis on naughty rather than nice. A few skeptics pulled his beard, others ran screaming in fear, and some were struck speechless in the overwhelming presence of the great Mr. Claus. There were the criers, the pants-wetters, the whiners and the demanders. Children who didn't know what they wanted, children who wanted everything, and parents who had waited on one line too many and were ready to take it out on anyone, Old Saint Nick being no exception.

If his little 'walk on the jolly side' served any purpose, it was to help him understand the haggard looks on the faces of his employees. And as for wanting to be a fly on the wall and listen to unsolicited comments about the store, he must remember in future to be careful what he wished for. Apparently, according to the mothers in line, Bryant's prices were too high and the clothing too, in the words of one customer, 'farty'. How in the world was he going to convey *that* comment tactfully to the buyers?

The end result was that Jason used his entire whopping fifteen-minute break entering notes and ideas for improvements into his organizer. Things like more cash registers, reserved time slots for seeing Santa and fashions that were...what exactly was the opposite of farty? Hip. Stylish. Phat? He'd have to ask one of the younger female sales associates for a term relevant to today's buyer.

Jason sighed. He was only in his thirties himself, but he was a man. He kept up with retail trends and he'd thought he had his finger on the pulse of the buying public, but apparently, he was falling short in women's fashions.

He had already taken the step to lure in younger female buyers by allowing the firemen from the charity calendar to play Santa at Bryant's for the week after Thanksgiving this year, as well as agreeing to host their charity bachelor auction and cocktail party at the store. Jason was on the board of directors of the local children's hospital and since the proceeds from the sales of the firemen calendar were going directly to the hospital, of course Bryant's would help promote it. And if events like the auction attracted a younger female consumer into Bryant's, it was a win-win situation for all.

But it appeared that simply luring a younger customer base into the store wasn't the problem, having something they'd be interested in purchasing, besides the hunky firemen, was. Jason would have to get out, shop the competition and see what was hot or Bryant's was a grand old lady doomed for failure.

Feeling rather less than jolly, Jason took his seat—actually, his golden red velvet throne—for the afternoon round of precious little ones. The coffee he'd consumed during his break hadn't helped revive him any, and he felt embarrassed for offering it up as inspiration to his employees that morning as if it was a cure all. Perhaps a bottle of Irish Whisky would work better. No, he could never actually do that, but at the moment, it was a tempting thought.

And then something even more tempting stepped into his view and he nearly pulled off his white wig and fake spectacles to make sure he was seeing correctly. Perhaps he was delirious because she cut in front of the line of kiddies still being held back behind the "Feeding the Reindeer—Back in 15 minutes" sign and perched her shapely behind right on his knee.

"Don't you look cute! Can I tell you what I want for Christmas?" She treated him to a gorgeous smile, followed by an immediate frown as she hopped back off his lap. "Oh my god! You're not Troy."

No, he wasn't, but right then, Jason sure wished he were. He did manage to shake his head to indicate to the woman that indeed, no, he was not Troy.

"I apologize. I must have gotten my signals crossed. I thought Troy O'Donnell was supposed to be here today."

He finally found his voice. "No apology necessary. Your friend," at least he certainly hoped they were only friends and nothing more, "was supposed to be here today, but he's ill."

She frowned. "Oh. I'll have to call him. But, I sat in your lap! I've gotten friendlier with you than I did with my last date. I'm so sorry." She cringed and covered her reddened face with her hands.

He stored away that information about her unfriendly last date for later use. "No apology needed for that either. Compared to what I've endured today, it was my pleasure." Jason smiled. His pleasure, indeed, he thought as he took in the tall strawberry blond and her bottomless blue eyes.

The woman of his future dreams stuck a hand out toward him. "I'm Troy's sister, Tessa O'Donnell. I don't recognize you from the fireman calendar. I was the photographer. Are you from the firehouse?"

He shook her warm hand and pondered his answer. "Um, no. The store brought me in last minute." There, that wasn't exactly a lie.

She smiled and shook her head. "I still can't believe stuffy old Bryant's is holding the Hunky Firemen Bachelor Auction here!"

Hmmm. Farty and now stuffy, too. Jason stifled a sigh. Instead, he opted for damage control. "I actually heard that the new COO is trying for a younger image for Bryant's."

Tessa screwed up her face. "The new COO is still a Bryant, isn't he? Born with a silver spoon in his mouth and a maid, nanny, butler, chauffeur and chef up his butt from the day he was born. I wish him luck, but I don't think there is any hope of changing Bryant's image after all these years, particularly for a man who has no clue what life is like in the real world."

Jason swallowed. She'd forgotten the private tutor and the gardener that came with his upbringing, and also that he'd moved out of the house—all right, mansion—the moment he was old enough to escape that life and prove to himself and his family he could make it in the 'real world'. But he had been born a Bryant and was now in charge of Bryant's. That would represent nepotism at its best in Tessa's eyes. Forget about the fact that he had worked his way up from the bottom to get where he was today, he was still his grandfather's heir and always would be.

She glanced over her shoulder at the growing line of irate mothers and irritated children that he'd been trying, and failing, to ignore as he concentrated on her. "Looks like the crowd is getting restless, so I better get to business before they rebel. I'm actually the photographer for the auction, too, so I came by to check out the site. I'm taking press shots for PR, they promised us coverage in the local paper." She frowned. "I'm sorry, I didn't catch your name."

"It's Ja...um, Jay Bee." He nearly groaned. He'd never been a good liar, particularly not on the fly.

She smiled and repeated, "JB. Nice to meet you. You better get back to work before the *big boss* fires you."

He nodded, noting that she said 'big boss' as if he was the big bad wolf, something to be both mocked and feared at the same time. Although he could live with JB. Better than his invention of Jay Bee, and it wasn't even really a lie, just his initials.

"Maybe I'll come back later and take some candid shots of you and the kids, if you don't mind." She raised a brow, waiting for his answer.

"Um, sure."

"Great." And with a wave and a smile, she was off, leaving Jason to slump in his throne. He groaned. The first female in a long time to make his heart beat faster, and she not only hated the real him on principal, but he'd already lied to her. It didn't bode well for their future romance. But he'd faced bigger dilemmas than this before, and a Bryant never gave up.

Chapter 2

Tessa walked away from the hunky Santa and nearly smacked directly into an elf on her way out of Bryant's holiday department. It had been a long time since just speaking with a man had affected her that way. Well, to be honest, she did more than speak; she'd sat in his lap! That wasn't too embarrassing.

The ringing of her phone in her purse disrupted any further thought of her embarrassment as she began the arduous battle to locate the miniscule device in the giant bag before it stopped ringing.

Just in the nick of time, she flipped it open. "Hello?"

"Tessa. It's Amy. Your brother is home sick. I wanted to call and catch you at home before you went over to Bryant's to take the pictures, but I've been so busy trying to take care of him all morning. Is he always such a stubborn ass when he's ill?"

Tessa let out a snort of a laugh. Her brother's fiancé had never had the pleasure of tending a sick Troy to date. "Oh, yeah. You should have seen him when we both had chicken pox. He tried to get out of bed to play football. Said the team needed him and they'd all had the chicken pox already anyway so it wouldn't matter. He actually snuck out of the house and got all the way down to the field before the coach sent him back home."

She heard Amy sigh. "Well, I think the worst of it is over. He hasn't thrown up in a little while and he actually managed to keep down some dry toast and tea, although you would have thought I was feeding him poison with the faces he was making over the tea."

Tessa laughed. "That sounds about right."

"He's still insisting on going down to Bryant's to play Santa today."

"Tell him don't bother. I'm here and I met his replacement. He's handling it just fine."

"That is so good to hear. Is it one of the other guys from

the calendar?"

"No. The store found someone to fill in." Tessa said a silent thank you that it wasn't one of the guys she'd photographed nearly naked for the Hunky Firemen Calendar. Given the fact that she had been the photographer for the calendar, it probably would have been pretty inappropriate and unprofessional to start dating one of them. And judging by the way all the firemen had steered a wide berth around her during the shoot, she strongly suspected Troy had stuck his nose in her business, yet again, and warned them to stay away from her.

But Troy wasn't here now, and JB was. Wouldn't a date with Mr. Claus be nice...

Wow. Where had that thought come from? She'd only just met JB and she was already thinking about *dating* him.

Unbidden, Tessa suddenly got a mental picture of JB without the Santa suit when Amy's voice came through the earpiece and interrupted her fantasy. "I will be sure to tell Troy they got someone else. You keep your phone on just in case he doesn't believe me and you have to back me up."

"He'll probably think we're both in on some great Santa Claus conspiracy together, but I'll do my best to convince him."

"Thanks. Oh, no. I gotta go, he's up and wandering around again."

Tessa laughed, said goodbye and hung up. Not envying Amy one bit, she continued on to the location for the bachelor auction.

Along the way, she let her hand glide over a cashmere sweater in a gorgeous shade of rich forest green. She still needed Christmas gifts for just about everyone on her list. The sweater would look great on Amy. Herself, too, for that matter.

She ran her hand down the sleeve, where it came to a dead stop at the price tag. Phew! Bryant's was definitely not the place for her holiday shopping. She shook her head at the thought of paying what was probably a week's salary for some people for a sweater. With one more wistful backward glance, Tessa stepped onto the escalator.

Ability to shop there or not, Bryant's was still a festive place to be. The store was all decked out, right down to the giant red bows printed on the white shopping bags the many customers were toting. The holiday spirit was kind of infectious and Tessa found herself humming along with the piped in seasonal music by the time she reached the next floor, which was supposedly her destination.

Frowning, she looked around at the white fluffy sea of wedding dresses surrounding her, then riffled through her bag to find the notes she'd taken regarding the charity bachelor auction. This was the place, Bryant's, third floor. She looked around again and saw the small stage and runway that ran down the center of the department in preparation for the upcoming event. This was definitely the place.

The auction was in a week, so unless some major merchandise reshuffling was going to be implemented and fast, it was more than likely that the hunky firemen and the hoards of women bidding on them would be surrounded by wedding dresses. Tessa thought it doubtful that a woman in the market for a man for the night would also be buying a wedding dress.

Okay, there would be one exception to that rule, her brother's fiancé. But Troy had only agreed to be in the calendar, and then later, some event planner came up with the idea for the guys to also be sold at auction to promote calendar sales and raise more money for charity. Officially, though engaged, Troy was unmarried and therefore eligible for auction. Amy was planning on buying him herself anyway since the money was for a good cause.

But Tessa would bet money of her own that Amy would be the only one attending interested in buying both a fireman (Troy) and a wedding dress (in which to marry Troy). It seemed like poor planning on the part of Bryant's management to have a captive audience of young, upwardly mobile women with money to spend stuck smack in the middle of a department full of merchandise they'd have no interest in purchasing.

Oh, well. Not her problem. Tessa pulled out her digital camera and lined up a few shots of the runway from different locations, trying to picture the room packed full of people. Maybe she should bring a ladder for the shoot. She had a feeling that if she wasn't actually on the stage with the guys, she wasn't going to manage to get anywhere near it. They were expecting quite a crowd. The sales for the calendar so far had already been huge, and it had only been on sale since the first of November. Less than a month and they'd actually already done a second print run to meet the demand.

Satisfied she had everything she needed—in the way of preliminary photographs anyway, her life was missing too many other things, a man included, to think about them all now—Tessa headed back downstairs. She wanted to see how Santa was doing with the kiddies, strictly so she could take some pictures for the paper, of course. She definitely wasn't hurrying toward the holiday department hoping to catch JB before he got off work for the day. She glanced at her watch. Exactly what time did Santa clock out? Good question.

Tessa found JB right where she'd left him, knee deep in children, literally. She still couldn't believe she'd actually sat on his knee. Although from what she could tell, it felt like a nice strong substantial knee, muscular but not too bulky, as if he was a runner, but not a body builder. And why was she obsessing over JB's leg muscles? It was probably leftover from photographing all those half-naked firemen a few months back. Kind of like looking at the menu and then leaving the restaurant without ordering, it's going to leave you a little hungry, particularly if you haven't eaten in a really, really long time.

Sighing, Tessa stared at the Santa she wouldn't mind letting slide down her...um, chimney. Jeez, she better get a hold of herself. She hadn't even seen him undressed yet. Blushing at her own thoughts, she corrected herself. She hadn't even seen him out of his Santa suit yet. Hmm. That sounded even cruder. Contemplating sex with Santa was too kinky for a former good little Catholic schoolgirl to even think about without saying a few Hail Mary's after.

And speaking of…between the good little boys and girls, Santa noticed her and smiled, his blue eyes twinkling as brightly as Clement Moore described in his poem about the big guy. JB turned his attention back to little whoever, listening to her as if she was the most important person in the world at that moment, and Tessa felt her heart do a little flip.

Camera armed and ready, she captured the moment. Santa's arrival at Bryant's was an annual tradition, and the local newspaper she sold photos to on a freelance basis would definitely use these shots in tomorrow's edition.

Tessa was still happily snapping away when an older woman in a green pantsuit with shoe-polish black hair and eyebrows not found in nature stepped into the shot. A small argument ensued, involving lots of head shaking on JB's part and much finger waving on hers. Tessa watched the woman stalk to the "Feeding the Reindeer-Back in 15 minutes" sign and plant it firmly in front of the next mother and child, which caused more animated debate amid those waiting in line.

Smiling, Tessa made her way over to JB. "What is she, the union rep?"

He glanced up and looked embarrassed. "Close. I seem to be taking a break. Would you like to join me in the restaurant for a quick bite?"

Tessa raised an eyebrow. Oh, boy. Was he asking her out? Too bad she'd have to burst his bubble with a slice of reality. "Have you been in the restaurant here during the holidays? Even if we could get a table, we wouldn't even get served in under an hour. According to the sign, you have only fifteen minutes."

JB looked surprised. "An hour? Really? Has that been your experience?"

"Yeah."

He frowned. "Hmm. Well, I…uh…work here. So I usually get served a bit faster. But still, something needs to be done about the wait for customers. I'll have to remember to…uh, tell my superiors."

Tessa made a derisive noise. "Well, I got a whole list of things you can tell them, but I doubt they'll listen to you. No offense." She hadn't meant to insult him, but really, how high up the corporate ladder could he be if he was playing Santa. He probably sold shoes or something.

Hmm, a hottie with a discount on shoes...

He raised a brow. "None taken. It sounds like you have a lot to say, more than I'll have time to absorb in just fifteen minutes. Maybe instead of lunch we should have dinner after I get off Santa duty tonight."

Santa Claus was hitting on her! And naughty girl that she was, she liked it. Sure that talking about how to improve the store was just an excuse to ask her out for dinner, she agreed. "I would love to discuss the store with you. What time do you finish here?"

He frowned slightly. "I'm not really sure. I'll have to ask somebody. Can I call you?"

She smiled. Now he'd asked for her phone number! Things were getting better all the time. She dug a tattered business card out of her purse and handed it to him. "That has both of my phone numbers and my email address."

He grinned. "Great." Then eyebrow lady came toward them and his face showed something close to fear. This woman must be somebody important the way he acted around her.

"Look. I see you're busy. I'm gonna go. I'll talk to you later?"

He looked relieved. "Definitely." Then he turned and intercepted dragon lady before she got any nearer to them.

Tessa smiled. It was good to see a woman in management respected by a male underling. It was about damn time. Feeling good for all womankind everywhere, she headed home to send off the Santa shots to her contact at the paper for tomorrow morning's edition and more importantly, find something to wear for her date tonight!

Chapter 3

"Were you flirting with that woman?" Peggy stood before him, hands on her hips, looking demanding.

He suddenly felt like his mother was interrogating him instead of just his administrative assistant. "I wasn't flirting. She's the photographer who shot your beloved firemen calendar that you drool over at every opportunity. She's also Mr. December's sister." He let that last bit of information drop casually.

Peggy's eyes flew open wide. "Really! Well, I wish you'd told me sooner. I would have asked her how he was feeling."

Jason smothered a smile. He had been flirting, but he knew the mention of her favorite calendar man would serve well to distract Peggy from the subject. She may know him well, but he knew her better.

A busboy from the store's restaurant walked up and handed Peggy a to-go container. She thrust it at Jason. "Go up to your office and eat this before you fall over! I know you haven't eaten all day."

He took the container. "I did so eat."

"Donuts and coffee in the break room don't count."

He groaned at being caught. "Come with me to my office. I have some things I want you to take care of while I'm finishing the day out as Claus."

Shaking her head, she followed him to his office, grumbling. "Stupidest idea I've ever heard of. COO and playing Santa Claus!"

"No, it wasn't. I've been enlightened to a number of issues today while out on the floor." He resisted the urge to add "in the war zone'. He loved the customers, he reminded himself, each and every grumpy one of them.

"Eat while you talk and I'll take notes." Peggy was probably the only assistant left in the country who still took steno—little brown flip notebook, indecipherable shorthand and all.

In his office, Jason pulled down the fake beard and opened the container. Tuna on whole grain toast with lettuce and tomato, his absolute favorite. Good old Peggy.

He took a nibble, chewed, swallowed and began to list his ideas for her. "First. I want someone to move in a display of impulse purchase items within reach of the Santa line immediately. The customers will be less bored in line if they can select their holiday cards or pick out their wrapping paper while waiting."

Peggy nodded approvingly. "Good idea. Get them while they're trapped and take their money."

He smiled at Peggy's raw honesty, but thanked god she rarely actually spoke with the customers directly. "Next…"

"Nah, uh. Take another bite first."

He rolled his eyes, took a bite of sandwich, chewed and swallowed again before he continued. "I want you to speak with the restaurant manager about improving service for the busy season. Maybe we can get those beepers so the customers can shop until we beep them when their table is ready. Bring in extra help for the kitchen and wait staff to speed service. Customers aren't spending money if they are sitting in the restaurant waiting an hour for their food to be delivered. Turning the tables faster will give the customers more time to shop and increase the amount of food sold."

Peggy nodded and continued to scribble. She didn't yell at him about eating again so he continued. "Also, see if the restaurant manager can come up with an idea for a reservation system to use for the Santa visits. Maybe people can sign up for a specific hour when they arrive at the store, go shopping, and then come back for their appointment."

He took another unsolicited bite and swallowed as his stomach started to feel less achy. Then he tackled the sticky subject. "Peggy. Is Bryant's out of style? As far as clothing, I mean."

She shrugged. "I don't think so. I like the clothes."

Hmm. That may be the problem. Peggy always looked professional in the attire she purchased at Bryant's, but she was a seventy-year-old secretary. She wasn't exactly wearing clothing from Bryant's to go out clubbing after work.

"I can see what you are thinking. What does an old lady know? But let me tell you something. I see what my son let's my granddaughter wear, ripped jeans with her thong underwear and ass crack showing, and I'd be embarrassed if Bryant's sold stuff like that. I don't care if it is supposedly in style. You have to draw the line somewhere. Doesn't class count for anything anymore nowadays?"

Jason sighed. "You're right. I can't picture us selling that kind of image either. But there has to be a middle ground somewhere. As soon as I can, maybe tonight, I'm going to start shopping some of the competition and see what ideas I can find."

"What about your date?"

He raised a brow. "How do you know about my date?"

"Good ears. And for your information, you get off at five tonight. That's when the next Santa comes in for the night shift. Antonio Sanchez. Mr. October and one hunk of a burning Latin lover from what I can see, and there was a lot to see, let me tell you! There was nothing between him and the camera but a happy looking pumpkin."

Jason laughed. "Great. Thank you, Peggy. I'll look forward to meeting him after that description."

"So where you taking Mr. December's sister?"

"I hadn't thought about that." He couldn't take her to his usual haunts and still maintain that he wasn't really Jason Bryant. He was too well known. The matre de's all greeted him by name. "Where would you go for a nice casual dinner?"

"On my salary, McDonald's. On your salary, Guido's in nice."

"On your salary, you could buy your own McDonald's and you know it. Can you make a reservation for me at Guido's, around seven for two people?"

"Sure."

"Oh, and make the reservation under my initials, JB."

Peggy narrowed her eyes. "Why?"

Time to pull rank. "Just do it, please."

She raised a brow, sarcasm dripping from her voice. "Yes, sir."

Feeling bad, he closed the to-go container, popped it into the tiny fridge behind his desk and stood. "Thank you, Peggy." To smooth things over, he dropped a kiss on the forehead of the woman who had been like a grandmother to him for years.

She rolled her eyes. "Sure, you charmer. Can't even stay mad at you..." Steno pad in hand, she stalked out his door, grumbling the entire way while Jason smiled.

One last piece of business to take care of before he went back to hell—make that the North Pole. Pulling out Tessa's card, he dialed the number and held his breath. Why he was so nervous he didn't know. She'd already said yes. But she'd said yes to JB, not Jason Bryant. Would the difference really matter to her? More importantly, exactly how far was he willing to go with this deception?

~

"Reservation?" The matre' de, swathed in black polyester, asked politely.

Guilt oozing from every pore, Jason answered. "JB. Table for two, I'm expecting a lady." He'd have to come up with a fake last name for himself if he was going to keep up this sham.

The man consulted a large leather-bound book on the podium and nodded. "The lady is already waiting for you at your table. Right this way."

Impressed with Tessa's promptness, he wondered if she was always this timely or if she was just anxious to see him. He knew which option he was hoping for.

He'd had her meet him at the restaurant because he drove a car that cost more than some people's homes and he was fairly sure it didn't fit the JB image he was reluctantly portraying.

Tessa's back was to him as he approached the table and he found himself anxiously holding his breath as he walked around to take his seat and face her.

"Hi! Good thing you made the reservations under JB. I don't even know your last name." She smiled brilliantly at him.

Still not having come up with a last name, and not really wanting to, he changed the subject. "You look...amazing." That, at least, was not a lie. With her hair pulled back into a sleek ponytail and wearing a black wool turtleneck mini-dress with knee-high red leather boots, Tessa had transformed into a classy but youthful, sexy siren. Pretty sure that there was some new term more appropriate than 'classy', Jason realized he really had to brush up on his fashion lingo.

Tessa was wearing more makeup than she had been at the store and her eyes looked brighter, her mouth fuller, more kissable. "Thank you." She accepted his compliment as embarrassed spots of red stained each alabaster cheek.

"Can I ask you a personal question?" He leaned forward in his chair.

Her eyes opened a little wider and she looked surprised. "Uh, okay."

"Where do you shop?"

Now, she really looked surprised. "For what?"

"Your clothes."

She leaned back in her chair. "Um. A lot of places. Why?"

"You are the perfect image for the new Bryant's customer."

Her face visibly fell.

"What's the matter? Did I say something wrong?"

Tessa swallowed hard as her heart fell to the pit of her stomach and she avoided JB's eyes. She knew she didn't have a poker face. Every thought showed immediately. It had been the bane of her existence since the time she was a child and it made lying, even in adulthood, impossible.

Knowing that, she still attempted it anyway. "No. No really. Everything is fine."

"No, it's not. I said something to upset you." He shuffled his chair around until he was sitting next to her, his knee bumping her leg as he laid one hand over hers. "Tell me."

She really thought she'd felt the vibe of mutual attraction from him today at the store. She was apparently mistaken. And he looked so yummy, too, all decked out in fitted trousers and a deep blue button down shirt that accented his eyes. She sighed, so much for her female intuition. Well-dressed, polite, handsome, he was probably gay and she was just too excited about him to realize it.

"It's stupid. I thought that talking about Bryant's was just an excuse to ask me out." In an attempt to lighten things up, she laughed. Feeling no lighter, she studied the tablecloth intently. "I'm fine, really. Just feeling a little silly. Go on. Scoot yourself back over to your side of the table. Take notes, whatever. I'll tell you anything you want to know."

When he didn't move, she glanced up and found his eyes narrowed and watching her. "No. I was stupid to assume that I could use this dinner to combine business with pleasure. But given the choice, when it comes to you, I'll take pleasure, fuck business."

Her shock over his unexpected profanity must have shown, and he shook his head. "I'm sorry. That was inappropriate."

"Well, as long as we're being inappropriate..." She couldn't help it, the draw to him was irresistible. Unable to stop, Tessa leaned forward and watched his shock as she touched her lips to his. His mouth felt as warm and inviting as it looked and she sank deeper into him.

She raised one hand and wrapped it around the back of his blonde head, tangling her fingers in the hair at the nape until he groaned...and the waiter cleared his throat.

"Can I get anyone a drink...or a room?"

They separated as fast as you might expect two people in their situation would.

JB recovered far quicker than she. He ran a hand over his lips, removing most of her lipstick and asked, "Did you get in any of the new Beaujolais Nouveau?"

The waiter sputtered for a moment and then answered. "I don't know."

"Could you please check and find out?"

Now it was the waiter's turn to look embarrassed. "I'll be right back."

JB turned back to her and smiled. He raised one hand and ran a finger down her cheek, which she was sure was crimson by now. Tessa wanted to crawl under the table and hide with embarrassment. "Maybe we had better talk business, Tessa. You're a little too tempting for me while we're in public."

If he only knew she was still tempted to crawl under the tablecloth but with him, and now it had nothing to do with embarrassment. She swallowed hard. "Thrift shop."

He raised a brow. "Excuse me?"

"That's where I buy a lot of my clothes. This dress is vintage from a thrift shop."

"Really?" He leaned back and looked at her appraisingly, reaching out a hand toward her hem. "May I?"

Not having a voice at the moment, and definitely not objecting to him fondling her or her clothing, she nodded.

His fingers brushed the fabric of the dress. "Good quality. Obviously timeless style." He shook his head. "Amazing. The boots?"

"New. I can't wear other people's footwear. Can't even go bowling, the shoes gross me out." Tessa watched in amazement as JB transformed from any woman's erotic dream into department store manager in the blink of an eye.

"You don't buy any clothes new?"

"Of course I do."

"Just not from Bryant's," he added.

She inwardly cringed, all right, maybe outwardly too. "I'm a freelancer. Bryant's is a little pricey for my budget."

"And not exactly your style," JB suggested.

She backpedaled. "Not necessarily. There are some things I like. Today, I saw a gorgeous cashmere sweater."

He nodded and she could tell he was preoccupied with thinking about something else by the distant look in his eyes. "What else. You said today you had a list of things you would change about Bryant's. Tell me."

The date had taken a few unexpected and not unwelcome turns already. What was one more? Tessa settled in for an evening of talking shop—or rather shopping—which was one of her favorite pastimes. Still, she hoped later for a night filled with her second favorite pastime, which would involve no talking at all.

She nodded and dove right in. "Okay. We've got to discuss all those wedding dresses on the third floor…"

He frowned and she smiled. A gorgeous man that kissed like the devil, liked clothes, listened to her when she talked, and knew about wine. Christmas had come early this year!

Chapter 4

"Mr. Bryant?"

"Hmm?"

"I asked you if we could go home now since it looks like we're done."

Jason noticed the sun rising through the window in the department. "Of course." He'd driven the crew straight through the night and into the next morning. "When are you scheduled in again, Jonathon?"

Jonathon glanced at his watch. "In about two hours."

Jason groaned. "I'm sorry. I can't even give you the day off. We're already short handed."

Jonathon smiled. "It's okay. If I can grab an hour nap, a shower and change my clothes, I'll be as good as new. And just think of my next paycheck with all this overtime! I'll be able to buy my girl something really nice for Hanukah."

Ahh, the exuberance of youth. Jason smiled. "Thanks, Jonathon. And tell the others thank you, also. Now get out of here."

Jason glanced around the former bridal department. Gone were the miles of white silk, satin and tulle, banished to a corner on the bottom floor behind the baby section, a more logical place for it anyway. He had no doubt that brides would find the department when they needed it. In its place on the sunny third floor was every item he could find in store stock that said young, fabulous female. And so Bryant's new department had been born, catering to women too sophisticated for the junior department but funkier than the misses department, just in time for the upcoming bachelor auction.

He shook his head. He should have thought of the change himself. Retail was his life, it was in his blood, and it took Tessa to open his eyes to how blind he was for holding the bachelor auction in the bridal department. His excuse was that the stage was already there from a recent bridal show.

His eyes had been opened to something else the night before, too. He realized as much as he wanted Tessa—and did he want her, more than he could quantify—he couldn't take their relationship to a physical level while he was still lying to her. He wasn't sure who had been more surprised when he'd come to that realization, himself or Tessa as he'd left her standing by her car in the cold restaurant parking lot.

Things might have been easier on both of them if they hadn't been getting very well acquainted while pressed up against her car at the time. He'd known he couldn't bring her home to have sex in his penthouse without blowing his cover. And he couldn't follow her to her apartment because she would have seen what kind of car he drove. The depth of the deception had stopped him cold in his tracks.

This was not going to be some one-night stand. He wanted a relationship with Tessa and starting it off with a lie was bad enough, but even worse would be sleeping with her before he confessed that lie.

Tell the truth and possibly lose her, or continue to lie and never be able to have her, the choices were not at all appealing. The whole situation was laughable. He'd heard of men exaggerating about how much money they made, or lying to make their career sound better, but Jason was probably the only man in history who was pretending to be less successful to get a woman.

Maybe he had underestimated Tessa. He should have told her who he was the moment she'd accused him—or rather accused Jason Bryant—of having been born with a silver spoon in his mouth and servants up his ass. They could have both had a good laugh. Maybe she would have gotten a little embarrassed, but then they could have moved on from there. But now, he was eyeball deep in a lie and he didn't know how to peddle out of it.

On top of everything, the store was opening in two hours and he had yet to get to sleep. Good thing he kept a razor and a change of clothes in his office. Peggy would have his hide if she realized he'd worked all night. The woman was like a bloodhound when it came to sniffing out lies. Good thing he wasn't dating Peggy! The absurdity of that thought made him laugh out loud with giddiness from lack of sleep. Bryant's on the Saturday after Thanksgiving on two hours sleep. It was going to be one hell of a day.

He only hoped Santa Claus showed up for work today. That would be all he needed. Ho, ho, ho!

~

"Jesus, Jason! Did you sleep here all night?"

His dream of being wrapped in Tessa's arms was rudely squelched by Peggy's screech. He popped his head up off the desk and feigned alertness. "No, of course not."

Peggy's skeptical scowl came into view as his eyes focused. He let out a deep breath and gave in. "I worked all night, I only slept here for a few hours."

After a loud Hmph! Peggy declared, "You are going to go home and get some decent sleep in a real bed."

He shook his head. "I have to set up a meeting with the buyers about an idea for a vintage inspired line of clothing. I have to shuffle around the sales associates. I made some major changes last night. There's a new department. I need to send out a memo to the marketing department and get signs made, ads have to be run..." Jason halted when a large and strangely familiar looking male suddenly appeared in the doorway behind Peggy, dwarfing her.

At Jason's frown, Peggy hooked a thumb behind her. "And you have to speak with Mr. December."

Ahh, of course. He hadn't recognized him with his clothes on. And then, through the haze of exhaustion, Jason realized that just hours before he'd had his tongue down Mr. December's sister's throat. He sat up a little straighter in his desk chair. This guy looked even bigger clothed and in person than he did shirtless in the calendar photo. Hmm. Maybe it was a good thing he'd been using a fake name to date his sister, although, how was big brother going to react to Jason's lying?

Troy O'Donnell, a.k.a. Mr. December came forward,

arm extended. Jason's heart thudded in his chest until he realized Troy was smiling and only wanted to shake hands. The thought of shaking hands left him momentarily staring at the other man and wondering if the stomach virus that afflicted him yesterday was still contagious. Jason would have to risk it or offend him, so he shook warmly, vowing to wash with anti-bacterial soap at the soonest opportunity.

"Mr. Bryant. I have to apologize for yesterday..." Mr. December began.

Jason held up a hand to stop him. "Really, no apology is necessary. We...uh...had no problem finding a last minute replacement." He widened his eyes and shot Peggy a look that he hoped said to keep her mouth shut about who that replacement was.

Troy nodded. "I know. My sister was here and was very impressed by him."

Really? Well. Good to know. His heart beat a little faster at the mention of Tessa. "Oh, was she?"

The fireman nodded. "Seems so, she went on a date with him last night. That's the other reason I wanted to stop in, besides apologizing. I wanted to meet this guy and make sure he's decent. You know, since it looks like my sister is going to be dating him. I thought maybe you could tell me about him."

Jason swallowed. Not only did Tessa have an extremely huge weightlifter of a brother, he was also a hyper-protective one.

"Peggy, could you excuse Mr. O'Donnell and I?" He had to give her credit, for once she did as he asked without argument, but he was pretty certain she would have her ear pressed up against the outside of his door.

Jason opted to keep the nice sturdy wooden desk between himself and the Hulk. "Please, Mr. O'Donnell, have a seat."

"Only if you call me Troy. Mr. O'Donnell is my father."

Jason released a short nervous laugh. "I understand exactly how you feel. I'm in the same situation right now, except is seems I am unable to escape from the shadow of my family name no matter how hard I try. That's how I got myself into a very sticky situation, Troy." Jason swallowed hard. "I'm hoping you'll help me get out of it."

Tessa's brother raised an eyebrow. "I don't know how I can help, but I'll try. You and Bryant's have been really good to us at the firehouse so whatever I can do..."

Jason wondered if he would feel so generous after the revelation and launched right into his confession, preparing to duck should a brawny fist come his way.

Instead of the dreaded show of violence, Jason was surprised that the conclusion of his story was greeted with Troy's deep stomach-clutching laughter.

He waited it out in silence until Troy caught his breath, wiped his eyes and said, "Oh, man. You are in deep shit."

Hmm. Perhaps Troy routinely laughed before he beat someone up, kind of a mental tactic. Not that a man that large needed mental tactics, physical ones probably worked just fine for him. "I know, and I am more sorry than I can say."

Troy laughed and shook his head. "Don't apologize to me. Tessa's the one you have to worry about."

Finally breathing again at the realization that he might not be flattened at the end of Troy's muscle-bound arm, Jason nodded. "All right. So how do I approach her to apologize? Flowers? Jewelry? Designer shoes? Groveling on hands and knees? Whatever it takes, I'll do it."

Troy let out a long loud breath through pursed lips. "Tessa hates nothing more than a liar."

"She seems to hate rich people also, which is how I got into this mess."

Troy shook his head. "Nah, uh. She may stand on her soapbox and preach about the rich and the poor, but she will not abide being lied to."

Realization sank in. "She's been hurt by a man who has lied to her, hasn't she?"

After a moment's hesitation, Troy said, "You'll have to

ask her about her personal life."

Jason cleared his throat. "Um, is his still alive and walking? The guy that lied to her."

Troy frowned, and then Jason watched realization dawn across his face. Troy smiled. "I usually don't have to resort to killing or maiming Tessa's boyfriends. Just threatening to is enough. Besides, she hates when I interfere in her love life, and Tessa is someone you don't want pissed at you. Believe me."

Jason cringed.

Troy grimaced and added, "Sorry, man. I'm just telling you the truth."

"That's all right. I made this mess, I'll have to figure out a way to clean it up."

Troy stood. "Yeah, well good luck with that. I gotta go get suited up for the kiddies."

Jason laughed. "Good luck to you with that!"

Troy's face lit up. "Eh, they taught us how to handle just about anything in Santa School."

Ah, ha. Santa School. No wonder Jason had been so unprepared for the experience.

Troy continued, "I'll be fine. I love kids. Can't wait for Amy to get these damn wedding plans wrapped up so we can get started on our own."

Jason frowned. "Wedding plans, huh? What about that? You're going to be in the bachelor auction, aren't you?"

Troy rolled his eyes. "Yeah, since I'm officially not married yet, the chief said I couldn't get out of it."

"If you don't mind me asking, how's your fiancé handling it?"

"Oh, she's fine with it. She's planning on buying me herself, especially since the money goes to the children's hospital."

"You look skeptical."

Troy laughed. "Amy doesn't know this but I, uh, used to date *a lot*."

"You're thinking there may be some old flames there

bidding against Amy?"

Troy shook his head and let out a breath of frustration. "God, I hope not. But yeah, I'm worried."

It did Jason's heart good to see Goliath worried, too. He cringed in a show of sympathy. "I'm sorry."

Troy shrugged. "Nothing you can do about it, but thanks. I'll see you later."

Jason nodded. "Sure. I'll be around if you need anything."

They shook hands again, two men against a world full of women. "Thanks." Troy paused in the doorway. "Oh, one more thing. Tessa goes absolutely insane if the guy doesn't call right away, I mean like the day after the date. I wouldn't wait too long to call her if I were you."

If Troy was giving him Tessa tips, he must have won sibling approval, which was fabulous. He wanted nothing more than to talk to Tessa, if only he knew what to say and more importantly, who he was going to be when he called. At that thought, he stifled a groan.

Chapter 5

It was nearly noon when Tessa picked up the phone in her apartment and dialed the number she'd found in the directory for Bryant's Department Store. She listened to the ring, once, twice, and then slammed the receiver down.

What was she doing? First, she didn't even know JB's last name or in which department he worked. Second, Tessa O'Donnell did not call a man the day after a date! Sure, she believed in women's rights as much as the next girl, but some things were sacred. When it came to women, men should hold open the door, change flat tires, kill spiders and be the first to call after a date.

She probably would have felt less up in the air about JB if things hadn't gone so strangely the night before. She loved eating dinner with him and discussing the store and so many other things. He was so passionate when he spoke and equally attentive when he listened. Speaking of passionate and attentive…he'd nearly left her melted in a puddle of hormones and desire in the parking lot after dinner.

Tessa let out a shaky sigh. *Left her* was the operative phrase. She didn't doubt that JB, who ate with the proper fork and with his napkin spread neatly in his lap, would also be the type to play the gentleman when it came to sex on the first date. But the attraction between them was undeniable and left her hot and bothered and very alone and awake in her bed until late into the night when she finally fell into a fitful sleep.

Last night's fantasies starring JB still fresh in her mind, Tessa grabbed her tote bag and camera equipment and decided to head to Bryant's. Troy was feeling better and playing Santa today. She could snap a few photos of him for the bachelor auction and calendar promotion. Yeah, that was a good idea. And maybe while she was there, she could wander around a few of the departments to see more of what Bryant's sold. Since that had been one of the main topics of conversation at dinner last night, her interest was piqued. Of course, if she happened to run into JB, that would be good, too.

When she arrived, Bryant's parking lot was packed, of course. '*Tis the season*, she thought as she was forced to play stalker and tail a woman walking with two armloads full of packages to her parked car. Tessa slapped on a little lipstick as she waited for the shopper to load her trunk and finally buckle herself in and pull out of the space.

Tessa realized she really should try to get at least some of her own shopping done soon herself. This madness was only going to get worse the closer it got to December twenty-fifth. If she weren't careful, she'd be at the mall at closing time Christmas Eve instead of at her parents' house for dinner.

She sighed. If only she was crafty, she could make all her own gifts, avoid the aggravation of holiday shopping, save a whole lot of money and have all her relatives be impressed with how creative she was. She wondered if she could learn to knit and whip out a dozen or so scarves in a month. She'd have to see if she could find instructions on the internet when she got home. She'd heard you could find information on how to make a nuclear bomb online; surely there was something about knitting a scarf on there, too.

Once parked and inside the store, Tessa's first stop was the North Pole to annoy her brother. She took her sisterly duties very seriously, and number one on the list was to be a pain in the ass to her big brother.

Unfortunately, when she arrived there, he looked so cute and happy surrounded by all the kids, she didn't have the heart to tease him. Hmm. When had she become such a softy? Perhaps it was that biological clock thing women talked about. Nah, it didn't feel like baby lust. More like just the generous spirit of the holidays infecting her, although she thought being an aunt might be cool. She'd definitely have to learn how to knit booties or a blanket by the time Amy got pregnant.

She snapped a few photos of Troy with the kids. Troy

noticed the flash and looked over. He smiled and waved as she wound her way behind the ropes and stood behind the big gold Santa chair. "I can read the article now. *Mr. December, who will be entertaining ladies of all ages at the Children's Hospital charity Hot Firemen Bachelor Auction, takes time to play Santa at Bryant's for some good little boys and girls.*"

He screwed up his face. "Yeah, great. Thanks for reminding me about that auction."

"Oh, come on. They are only making you walk down the runway shirtless. At least they're letting you wear your pants. And considering you had such a hissy fit and refused to wear the strategically placed Santa hat I suggested for your calendar page, I would think you'd be happy about that."

"Yeah, that Santa hat was a real great idea. Thanks a lot for suggesting it."

"Hey, all the other guys were naked. And as much as I so didn't want to see my own brother like that, I figured it would look funny if you were the only one all covered up in a ski parka or something! Besides, the way you lift weights, I thought you would be dying to show off your body. You got it, might as well flaunt it, muscle man."

Troy rolled his eyes. "Well, I don't see you flaunting anything. When I do, then you can talk! Actually, scratch that. I had better *not* catch you flaunting anything! What are you doing here anyway, besides bothering me?"

She shrugged in what she hoped was a casual way. "Oh, you know. Taking a few photos, doing some shopping, maybe I'll visit JB."

Troy suddenly got very interested in the line of children. "Okay, well, have fun. I've got things to do, kiddies to see."

She looked at him surprised at the sudden brush off. "All right. See you later."

"Sure. Fine. Bye."

Hmph. Men were just too strange. It didn't matter whether they were brothers or boyfriends. Why women bothered with them, she really had no idea. Then she thought back to JB's kisses and decided that maybe some men, and some things you could do with them, might be worth the trouble.

Hmm. Now where to start her search... JB had been very interested in ladies clothing during their dinner last night. Since she was sure he wasn't gay and dressing in drag, judging by a certain bulge she'd accidentally bumped into while they were kissing against her car, she figured the interest must come from his work. She'd check the women's clothing departments first.

But search as she might, she didn't see hide nor hair of JB. Tessa had been through the Juniors, Misses, Plus Sizes and Petites and was about to give up when she decided to swing upstairs and take a quick look in Bridal. She was running out of options. He had definitely said he was working today, so he had to be somewhere.

She was considering how she might have missed him in one of the departments while he was on a break or something when she got to the top of the escalator on the third floor and literally stumbled off.

Gone was the Bridal Department and in its place was an entirely new display of women's wear. But gee whiz, when had this happened? It wasn't like this yesterday afternoon.

Tessa wandered to a rack and flipped through. The clothes weren't bad. Actually, they were pretty great, and every rack had a twenty percent off sign on it. She was reaching out for another hanger when she remembered what she said to JB at dinner and her hand stopped in mid motion. *We have to talk about all those wedding dresses...*

Holy crap. He'd done this overnight. But how? She considered this and came to the conclusion that the only explanation must be that JB was not as low on the Bryant's totem pole as she first assumed.

"Hello! Welcome to '*The Place to B*'." A perky, platinum and painfully young salesgirl pointed to the computer-generated sticker on her chest that read the name of the department. Tessa assumed *B* was some marketing gurus idea at being clever and short for Bryant's. "In honor of our newest women's department, everything on this floor is twenty percent off this weekend only. Please let me know if I can help you with anything."

"Actually..." Tessa held up one hand before the girl bopped off. "I was looking for one of your co-workers. His name is JB."

The girl frowned. "JB? Do you know his last name?"

Tessa sighed. She'd had her tongue in his mouth but still didn't know his last name, but she decided to keep that piece of information private. "No, I'm sorry I don't. I think he's in management. In fact, he may be in charge of this department."

The girl tapped her manicured finger lightly against her chin as she thought. "Well, there's Jonathon, but I've never heard anyone call him JB before. He's right over there with his girlfriend."

Tessa's stomach clenched as she spun to follow the girl's finger. She'd had a boyfriend cheat on her before. It was something you never recovered from and definitely something she never wanted to repeat again. If JB had a girlfriend and was all over her last night...

Her glance finally landed on a guy and girl, giggling in the corner and Tessa let out a breath she hadn't realized she'd been holding. Relief overwhelmed her when she discovered that Jonathon was definitely not JB. She swallowed and tried to calm her racing heart. "No, not him."

"Hmm." Blondie considered some more. "Maybe those are his initials?"

"I would assume so. I doubt his mother named him with two letters." The girl was trying her best to be helpful, she couldn't help it if she was both perky and blonde. Tessa reminded herself to try and be polite as her cell phone rang in her pocket.

She located the phone just as Blondie stuck one finger in the air and got an expression on her face that practically said

Eureka! "I know who has those initials!"

Tessa stopped her with one raised finger of her own as she answered the phone. "Hello?"

She smiled and her heart pounded a little faster, but in a good way when JB's rich voice came through her earpiece. "It's JB."

In a much better mood now, she smiled graciously at the salesgirl. Tessa covered the phone and whispered, "I found him. He's on the phone. Thank you so much for your help anyway."

"Sure, anytime." The girl nodded and ran off to answer the store phone, which had just started ringing at the nearest cash register.

She turned her attention back to JB. "Hi." When had her voice gotten so breathless?

He answered, "Hi, yourself. Where are you?"

"At Bryant's. Where are you?" Tessa moved over toward the window for some imagined privacy in the crowded store.

"What a coincidence. I'm at Bryant's, also."

"Then why aren't we together?" That was very flirtatious of her, but she was feeling pretty flirty at the moment.

He laughed. "I'd like nothing better, but I'll be stuck in meetings for most of the day. Can I see you tonight?"

Yay! Exactly the words she was hoping to hear. "Okay. When and where?"

"You pick it. Anywhere you want."

"My apartment, seven, I'll cook for you."

There was silence on the other end.

Quick to assume the worst, Tessa let insult take over. "I can cook, you know. My mother makes the best Irish stew you've ever tasted, and Shepard's pie and…"

"I believe you. I never insinuated that you couldn't cook. I'm sorry. Something here distracted me. Your place at seven would be wonderful. What can I bring?"

"A bottle of wine?"

"You got it. Give me the address, then I'm afraid I have to dash off."

She did and then hung up, feeling all giddy like a schoolgirl on her first date. Maybe she'd even treat herself to a hot new date outfit from the new department for twenty percent off. More importantly than that, she needed to hit the lingerie department, too. That area of her wardrobe was sorely lacking and could definitely use some new additions, especially in light of her date tonight. At least one thing was certain; with them dining at her apartment, there was no way he'd be able to leave her in the parking lot tonight!

One hour, two shopping bags and way more money than she should have spent later, Tessa and her wicked purchases made a wide berth around Troy in the Santa zone. Somehow she was afraid he'd sense what naughty lingerie she had in her bags, and she didn't need his interference to squelch her excitement. She rushed home to cook, clean and get sexy. Tonight was going to be special. She just knew it.

Chapter 6

Jason rubbed his face with his hands, feeling bone-deep tired and dreading his date with destiny, and Tessa, with every passing hour. He knew he would have to tell her this evening.

If she'd chosen a restaurant for their date, he probably wouldn't have confessed tonight. This was not a secret to be revealed to a reputedly hotheaded woman in public. But alone with her at her apartment, where she could yell and throw things at will, he had no excuse not to tell her. That is, no excuse except for the fact that he just plain didn't want to tell her. It would most likely mean losing her.

Dammit. It was too soon to lose her. He'd hardly had time to enjoy being with her. Although, was there ever a good time to lose something or someone you cared about?

"What's the matter, James Bond? All this intrigue catching up with you?"

He glanced up through splayed fingers. "Oh, Peggy. I'm sorry I had to drag you into this mess today."

She dismissed him with a wave of her hand. "Eh, don't worry about it. Most excitement I've had in years. Besides, I enjoyed watching that young salesgirl scurry for her phone and then sending her off on a wild goose chase for queen-sized footless tights!"

Jason shook his head. He was very glad Peggy was enjoying herself, because he sure wasn't. He'd nearly had a heart attack when he'd gotten off the elevator and saw Tessa speaking with one of the salesgirls—in the new department he'd created overnight based on her suggestions, no less. If *that* miraculous feat didn't tip her off as to his real identity, he didn't know what would.

He'd called Tessa's cell phone while Peggy had called the phone at the register and luckily, it seemed he'd managed to separate the two women before Tessa figured it out. He let out a sigh. *"Oh what a tangled web we weave..."*

"Oh, no. Now you're quoting Shakespeare, you must be

delirious. Go home and take a nap before your date," Peggy ordered.

Jason blew out a long slow breath and glanced at his watch. "No time to nap. I have to shower and change and she lives all the way across town. Don't worry about me. I'm sure it will be an early night. The minute I tell her who I really am, she'll throw me out."

Peggy raised a brow silently. He'd known she wouldn't like it when he told her about the lying. He'd been right.

Jason frowned at her. "Stop that."

"Stop what?"

"Judging me."

"*Judge not lest ye be judged.* See, I can quote literature, too."

"That's the Bible."

"The Bible is literature."

He let out another tired sigh and stood. "I better go."

"Have a good night." Even Peggy's 'good nights' seemed to have an element of sarcasm within them.

The only answer he could manage was a groan.

~

Jason could select a good wine in his sleep. That was exactly the problem, he was on the way to his date and nearly asleep on his feet. So tired, he'd almost forgotten to stop at the wine shop before driving to Tessa's.

Planning a date tonight with two hours sleep over the past two days was probably a bad idea. Especially since he needed to be in top form when he confessed his little deception to her and tried to convince her to not hate him for it. Hmm. Oh, well, hindsight was twenty-twenty and all that.

Not knowing what Tessa was serving for dinner, Jason picked out both a red and a white wine from the shelves of the liquor store down the street from his apartment and then headed over to her place. He hoped if she was going to throw her glass of wine at him after he told her, she was at least drinking the white for the sake of his linen shirt.

He didn't worry about her seeing his overpriced car

tonight, the jig would be up soon anyway, so he pulled right into a spot in front of her building and parked. It was a decent neighborhood, not rich, but not poor either, and the normalcy of it made his penthouse in his building, private elevator, doorman and all, seem a bit ridiculous. Maybe he did deserve all the derogatory comments she'd made the day he met her. Jeez, had that only been yesterday? It seemed far longer.

He found his way to her apartment without any trouble and rang the bell. But when Tessa answered the door, she surprised the hell out of him. Everything she was wearing was from the new department at Bryant's. He must have been staring because she commented on it.

"I took advantage of your twenty percent off sale. How the hell did you put that department together overnight?"

He smiled and handed her the paper bag with the wine as she moved back so he could step inside. "We worked until dawn."

Tessa put the bag down on the kitchen counter. She looked at him and then dropped eye contact, studying his shoes, the floor, anything except his face as she asked, "Is that why you left so quickly last night?"

"There were actually a few reasons why I left last night, but not one of them was because of you." He stepped closer, kissed her forehead and moved to take the wine out of the bag. "What are we having? Red or white wine?"

She looked a bit happier when she answered, "Dinner is chicken parmagiana with pasta and broccoli rabe in garlic and oil."

He raised a brow. "Is that your Irish mother's specialty?"

"No, it's mine. I waited tables at an Italian restaurant to pay for college. I picked up a few cooking tips in the kitchen."

Hmm. His trust fund and the fact that his grandfather had built the campus library had paid for his Ivy League education. Though Jason did work in the stockroom at Bryant's during summers all through high school. That had to count for something on the 'normal guy' scale, no?

Think about that later, a voice whispered in his head. *Enjoy the moment while you still can.* "So, chicken but with red sauce. We can go either red or white wine. Which do you prefer?"

She laughed. "Not being the connoisseur you are, I usually drink red in the winter and white in the summer. I'm sure that is appalling to you and totally wrong, but…"

"Not at all. The first rule of wine is to drink what you enjoy, no matter what the so-called experts say." He would just have to dodge any flying red wine that came his way…or get a new shirt. He accepted the corkscrew she handed him and opened the bottle of Shiraz. "You look great, by the way."

"Thanks." She handed him two wine glasses. "Where did you get all those clothes for the new department on such short notice?"

"That's the interesting part. Every item was already on the racks elsewhere in the store. Things that were lost in the other departments made a great statement after I pulled them out and put it all together." He shrugged casually. Maybe the buyers weren't the problem after all. The problem was in the display, and that was partially his own fault for not spending more time out on the floor.

"It sure did make a statement. I loved everything. It was hard to choose what to buy."

He let his gaze roam over her oversized cardigan and skinny pants tucked into high boots. "You chose well."

It was far too easy to make her blush. He realized he liked it as he watched her cheeks color when she accepted his compliment. "Thanks. So your bosses must be impressed with you."

Jason took a deep steadying breath. "Actually, about that…"

A loud buzz from the kitchen area startled him enough that he nearly sloshed the garnet-colored wine out of his glass and onto her beige carpet.

Tessa held up one hand. "Hold that thought. The chicken is done. Why don't you have a seat at the table and I'll serve us."

Literally saved by the bell. This must be what prisoners who get an eleventh hour stay of execution from the governor feel like. "Sure." He took his seat, as well as a large swallow of wine.

She served, they ate, and he had to say, Tessa was a great cook and dinner was excellent. He was definitely glad he waited until after they'd eaten to think about confessing again. The fact that they had polished off the entire bottle of wine between them couldn't hurt his cause one bit. Sated with both wine and comfort food, Jason decided to wait just a little bit longer before he spilled the beans and ruined the perfect evening.

He was rehearsing possible confession scenarios in his head as he helped clear the plates, but she insisted he sit down and relax on the couch while she made the coffee and got dessert together. Any excuse to procrastinate further was fine with him, so he agreed heartily. His mind was made up, he'd confess right after coffee and dessert. He did as he was told and sat.

The couch, which he swore was the softest and most comfortable one he'd ever sat upon, swallowed him up. He was now full and exhausted, so he decided to close his eyes, just for a moment while he waited for Tessa...

And that was the last thing he remembered until sunlight streaming in from the living room window woke him the next morning.

Jason sat up and the wool throw Tessa must have put on him the night before fell to the floor. He groaned. Falling asleep and spending the night on her couch hadn't been his plan. It's not like he exactly had a good plan, but this definitely was not it.

"Good morning." Tessa wandered out of the bedroom looking warm, tousled and sexy as hell even in sweats.

He groaned. "I am so sorry."

Laughing, she walked to the kitchen and he realized he smelled fresh brewed coffee. "Don't be silly. You were exhausted. It's fine. Coffee? I set the timer last night before I went to bed." She held up the full pot.

"God, yes." The smell must have been what woke him.

"Milk, sugar?"

"Black."

She delivered the blessed beverage and perched next to him on the edge of the couch, sipping from her own mug. He took a long slow sip and closed his eyes. "Thank you."

"You work too hard. You need a day off." Then she frowned. "You don't have to work today, do you? It's Sunday."

He laughed. "Weekends and holidays in the retail business only mean that you have to work harder. During the holiday rush, I usually try to take off a day during the week, unless there's a special sale going on."

She looked a bit saddened. "What time do you have to go in?"

Here was one area where being the boss actually paid off. "I don't have any meetings scheduled this morning, so I guess I can go in late if I want to."

She put her mug down on the table and looked pleased. "Good. Stay for breakfast. Dessert last night was going to be crepes stuffed with marscapone cheese and fruit. They'll make a pretty good Sunday brunch, I think."

Brunch with Tessa. Visions of the perfect Sunday morning filled his head. Waking up with Tessa warm in his arms, drinking coffee, reading the fat Sunday paper, eating brunch, rolling back into bed with her for a little…

He swallowed and his gaze dropped momentarily to her lips. When he raised his eyes again, he saw she was watching him closely. Tessa took his mug right out of his hand and put it on the table next to hers and then leaned in.

It took all of his strength to lean away from her, but he somehow managed it. Her eyes narrowed, but she stayed close. "What's wrong?"

"Tessa. You don't know me very well."

"Okay, fine. Let me get to know you. Are you married?"

"No."

"Children, in or out of wedlock?"

Jason shook his head. "No."

Tessa pursed her lips and considered. "Convicted felon or murderer?"

He laughed. "No."

"Infected with AIDS, herpes or any other incurable sexually transmitted disease?"

"Definitely no." In light of all the things she'd mentioned that he could be, the fact that he was rich now seemed pretty silly actually.

She raised a brow. "You just don't want to kiss me?"

What could he say? Lies had gotten him into this mess, time for the truth. "I want to kiss you more than anything in the world."

"Me, too." She smiled and leaned in again, and this time he didn't pull away.

He barely had time to register that she tasted like sweetened coffee when she tangled her hands in his hair and pulled him down with her onto the couch.

Oh, man. His willpower was not that good. Definitely not good enough to be on top of a warm, soft Tessa and not react to it. He ran a hand down her soft cotton sweatpants and then up over her thermal shirt. To hell with lingerie, plain cotton had never felt so good.

He slipped a hand under the shirt and brushed the side of her bare breast with his hand. Discovering she wore no bra, he groaned.

She started to unbutton his shirt, and he was letting her, in spite of his resolve not to do this prior to telling her the truth. But by now his body was too into it to care that his mind objected.

Then, thank god, the phone on the table next to him rang.

He leapt off of her and sat back on the couch, trying to

catch his breath. That was a close call. He leaned further back so she could reach across him for the cordless phone and then he quickly slunk off to the bathroom.

Saved twice within twelve hours by loud ringing appliances. Perhaps fate was intervening on his behalf? First, last night when the oven timer went off just as he was about to confess, and now, when the phone rang just when he was far too tempted to resist her.

Maybe fate was telling him he wasn't meant to have sex with Tessa. But by the same logic that meant that he wasn't supposed to tell her the truth, either. He laughed at himself. Nice thought, but what exactly could he do, legally change his name to JB and move them both to another city where no one would recognize him?

All he knew was that every day that passed and he didn't tell her she would see as a betrayal when he finally did confess.

Fate or not, he knew deep down he could definitely not allow himself to make love to her. Not while he was still lying to her. With that thought, he swore to himself, no matter what happened with Tessa and this messy situation he'd created, he would never, ever lie again. It was just too much damn work.

Chapter 7

Of all of the times for Troy to call, it had to be now? Tessa sighed when she heard her big brother's voice. She should be sunk deep in between JB and the sofa enjoying a little pre-brunch tidbit and instead, she was on the phone.

She watched as JB, looking disheveled and yummy, skirted around her and disappeared into the bathroom. She tried to listen to Troy, but instead found herself picturing herself and JB naked in the shower together. But when JB reappeared and dove right for his overcoat, about to leave, her little fantasy was shattered.

"Hold on a second, Troy." She covered the mouthpiece of the phone. "Are you leaving?"

"I really have to go." JB planted a quick kiss on her mouth and whispered, "I'll call you later." Then he was gone.

Damn. Since when did guys play hard to get? It was all Troy's fault! As the door closed behind JB, Tessa launched into a rant directed right at her brother. "What exactly do you want that you had to call so early on a Sunday morning?"

"Hey, don't take your PMS out on me! And what was all that about?" Troy let out a sound of surprise. If there had been a light bulb above his head, Tessa imagined it would have lit up at that moment. "Is there somebody there with you?"

Nosy, interfering…"I don't see how that is any of your business but yes, perhaps I did have company for breakfast, until you interrupted us. I have a social life, too, you know." It was amazing she'd even gotten a date for the prom in high school. Troy was always scaring the boys away. "Well, aren't you going to demand to know who he is, what he does, get an IRS and FBI check on him?"

"No."

What? "No?"

"Actually, I've already met him and I approve. I'm glad

you two worked things out."

Worked things out? Hmm, it was always best to play more informed rather than less in situations such as this. Left to his own devices, Troy would spill more than if she questioned him. "Ah...yeah, me, too. But I can't believe you talked to him and didn't even tell me," Tessa said vaguely, hoping Troy would elaborate.

"Hey, it was a man to man confession type thing. And the poor guy was really torn up about lying to you."

Tessa's heart stopped. Lying about what? It couldn't be anything really bad or Troy would be angry and JB would have at least had one black eye, if not been in the hospital in traction.

Troy continued merrily on. "But even you wouldn't be enough of a bitch to not forgive one of the most eligible bachelors in the city. I figured the promise of designer footwear at cost would probably be enough to get you over the fact that he didn't tell you his family owns Bryant's."

Realization struck her like a lightening bolt. JB, B as in Bryant. Then she remembered the look on his face when she blurted out that the Bryant heir was probably born with a silver spoon in his mouth...as well as the other less pleasant and far from complimentary things she had added. She let out a big breath. Why in the world had he even asked her out after that insult in the first place? That was the question of the hour.

She made a beeline for the computer and booted it up.

"Tess?"

"Ah, yeah. Sorry." She typed 'Bryant' into Google and up popped more than she needed to confirm her suspicions, including a photo of Jason Bryant the first shaking hands with Jason Bryant the third as he took over the family legacy from the store's founder, his grandfather.

Troy was talking again. Damn it. This was no time for multi-tasking. "...wanted to know if you'd like to come to dinner."

"Can I get back to you?"

"Sure. I have to go in for my last Santa shift at Bryant's today, so dinner wouldn't be until about seven anyway."

"Okay. Thanks. I gotta go."

She could almost hear his smirk. "I'm sure you do. Say hi to Jason for me."

Tessa hung up, wondering when the universe had shifted and left Troy as the more knowledgeable sibling. How could she not have realized? There were so many signs. JB's—rather Jason's—impeccable clothing which probably cost more than her first car. His obsession with Bryant's and women's fashions. The fact he could rearrange an entire floor of the store on a whim overnight. She sat suddenly back in the desk chair. *Oh my god!* And, the fact that he wouldn't sleep with her.

Bingo! It wasn't that he didn't want to; it was because he was lying to her about who he was. He was being honorable. She let out a big sigh of relief. Her women's intuition wasn't that off kilter after all. The attraction she felt between them was real. She'd just have to work on her powers of observation and pay more attention to details from now on. Phew. That was a relief.

And now that the secret was out, a whole world of possibilities opened up to her. One of the most eligible men in the city was interested in her? Tessa O'Donnell! And he was sweet, hard-working, handsome and unbelievably hot and not at all snobby like she'd foolishly assumed someone like him would be. The whole situation didn't seem like it could be real. At least, not really happening to her. If she still couldn't taste him on her lips, she'd think it was all a dream.

But now, what was she going to do about it? She could play dumb and wait for him to tell her the truth. Sitting around and waiting really wasn't her style. She could take matters into her own hands. Yeah, that could be the way to go.

She hopped up from the computer and headed for the shower as a plan that had her heart throbbing (in addition to other parts of her) began to form.

~

Jason spent the morning trying and failing to keep his mind on work. Luckily nothing pressing demanded his attention, because with Tessa on his mind, he doubted he could have handled it. Knowing Troy was Santa again for the day, Jason avoided the holiday department like the plague. He spent most of his time in the new department, trying to get a feel for the customers' reactions to it.

As usual, time spent on the sales floor left him with a hundred ideas, so he grabbed a sandwich and headed for his office to enter them all into his organizer while he ate. Peggy, who had the day off, would have been extremely proud of him for remembering to eat all on his own.

With a smile on his face at that thought, he opened his office door and stopped dead in the doorway. Nearly dropping the sandwich, he placed it on a small table by the door and glanced up again to be sure he wasn't hallucinating.

Tessa stood before him in nothing but an open trench coat, high heels and extremely sexy lingerie. Bryant's lingerie, if he wasn't mistaken. He swallowed hard. "Tessa." His voice was so breathy, he wasn't sure it even carried as far as the desk, where Tessa was now perching her perfect behind and leaning back on her arms, thrusting her barely covered breasts out at him.

"Hi." She was sounding pretty breathy herself. His chest tightened, and so did parts lower.

"What are you doing here?" A half naked girl was draped on his desk and he stood frozen with guilt and asked her why. This lying stuff really sucked.

"Finishing what we started this morning."

Holy! This was a side of Tessa he hadn't seen before. He swallowed. "Um, this morning was probably a mistake. We need to talk about something first."

She raised a brow, and also one knee as she ran the toe of one stiletto up and down her opposite leg. "Come over here and we'll talk."

Somehow he doubted that. When he still didn't move,

102

she stood, slid the coat off until it landed in a heap at her feet and started to close the distance between them. Torn between running out of the door and closing it in case anyone should come into the office, he chose the latter, strictly to avoid embarrassment, of course.

She smiled and ran a hand up and down his chest. All right, so closing the door had been a mistake. Lesson learned. He grabbed her hand as it began to run back and forth just beneath his belt. "Tessa."

"Aren't you attracted to me?"

He swallowed audibly and held her as far away from him as the length of his arms would allow. "You know I am. But there is something I have to tell you, and it may affect how you feel about me. I can't go any further with you until you know the whole truth."

She smiled slyly. "What truth is that, *Jason?*"

He was just trying to figure out what to say when the fact that she had called him by his real name struck. His eyes widened. "You know?"

She nodded and reached up to touch her lips to his. He groaned and pulled her body closer before breaking away to ask, "And you're not angry?"

Her hands snaked around behind him and roamed below his belt to cup his buttocks. "Does it look like I'm angry?"

He closed his eyes as she pressed closer against him. "Troy had me terrified you'd never speak to me again after I told you."

"Never listen to Troy." She nibbled on his chin, and then moved to his ear, making him shiver.

"Oh, god, I want you." He ran his hands down her silk and lace clad body. He'd have to congratulate the lingerie buyers on their fine purchases. Jason took a deep breath. "But we can't do this here."

Tessa reached behind him and flipped the lock on the door. "Now we can. Besides, it's kind of always been one of my fantasies. Sex in an office on a big desk while everyone else is working and doesn't know."

He raised a brow and began backing them both up toward the desk. One of her fantasies, huh. That was really all he needed to hear. But the knock that sounded on the door was definitely not something he wanted to hear at that moment.

They both froze, two children caught with their hands in the cookie jar, except Jason's hand was currently somewhere where there weren't any cookies.

"Jason? You in there?"

"It's Troy!" Tessa hissed.

He held one finger to her lips. "Shhh. I know. Maybe he'll go away."

The handle jiggled on the door—thank god Tessa had locked it—and then there was silence.

Jason stifled a giggle. "I feel like a teenager."

"Me, too." Tessa laughed, but the look in her eyes was far from funny. "Kiss me."

"My pleasure."

Jason lowered his head to explore inside her mouth while Tessa's hands made short work of his belt and fly and began to explore inside his boxers.

He wanted more and laid her back on his desk. His mouth found her breast and he feasted while his fingers made their way to the wet heat between her legs.

He teased her, making small circles with his fingers until she writhed on the desk beneath his hand. "Jason. Make love to me."

His breath caught in his throat at the request, but he nodded.

Jason knew he'd never be able to sit at that desk again without remembering sliding into Tessa. Even the fact that he was standing with his pants down around his ankles didn't take away from how amazing it felt to be inside her, her legs wrapped around him, the feel of her heels digging into his buttocks as he plunged into her, how she shuddered and cried out his name when she came.

His name had never sounded so good in his ears, and he

came himself with a deep shudder and a sigh of absolute and utter satisfaction.

She clung to him afterwards as he held her close, kissing her face and feeling grateful for small blessings. "I'll never lie to you again. I swear."

She smiled at him devilishly. "You better not, or my big brother will beat you up."

Jason let out a nervous laugh. "That's not funny. Particularly after he almost caught us just now."

"Don't worry, he didn't hear. Besides, he told me he likes you."

"That's very good to know." Jason kissed her one last time before retrieving his pants and then bent to get her coat. "Let me grab something off the sales floor for you to wear home under this coat."

Tessa shrugged. "I drove here like this. I can drive home like this, too. What difference does it make?"

"What if you get pulled over?"

"I'm more likely to get out of the ticket wearing this than clothes, don't you think?"

He frowned and indicated her revealing underwear with the sweep of one hand. "*This* is only for me from now on. I'll pay your ticket if you get one. You keep covered up. Understood?"

She rolled her eyes. "Yes, sir. Sheesh, no wonder Troy approves of you."

Knowing that Troy liked him made him extremely happy. Jason had every hope of being around Tessa and her family for a very long time, besides the fact that Troy could probably level him with one well-placed punch.

He grabbed her jacket lapels and pulled her toward him for one more possessive kiss. "You have a problem with me thinking of you as mine?"

She shook her head. "No."

He smiled. "Good." He was just thinking that was fortunate because he was definitely planning on her remaining his when her cell phone rang. Again with the ringing! Now what did fate have to say?

While Tessa dug in her purse to find it, Jason shook his head. "At least we got to finish this time."

She smiled and answered the phone. "Troy! Um, hi. What's up?"

Jason finished tucking his shirt back into his pants and retied his tie as Tessa made the usual one-sided phone responses and then hung up. He glanced up and found her face bright red.

"What did he say?"

"He said in high school he used to date a girl who worked here and if we are going to have sex in the store, the janitor's closet off the storeroom on the third floor is a bit more private and soundproof."

Jason's hand slipped as he raised the knot up to his neck and he nearly choked himself with his own tie. "He heard us?" Uh, oh. Although he couldn't help but wonder which salesgirl it had been in the closet with Troy.

"He also asked if you wanted to come with me to his and Amy's apartment to have dinner tonight."

"Is he going to hit me?"

"No."

"How can you be so sure?"

"Because he told me to tell you he wasn't going to punch you, but you were going to have a nice long talk about our future."

Jason laughed. Tessa in his future he could handle. "All right."

Tessa's face broke into a gorgeous smile.

Jason frowned. "What?"

"You are the first man ever that Troy has wanted to have a long talk with about my future."

"And this is a good thing?"

"Oh, yeah. This is a very good thing." Tessa grabbed him by his newly knotted tie and kissed him deeply, and that was definitely a good thing.

The End

CAN'T BUY ME LOVE

Chapter 1

"No one at the party thought the cake looked anything like my little Isabella."

"Mrs. Steinhoff. It was a cake. I made it look as much like your poodle as I could, but it was still a cake. I can only do so much." A cake for a birthday party for a freaking poodle and the woman was giving her grief over it? Zoey Massey ran a hand over her temple, trying to massage away the ache that had resided there non-stop all day.

"Well, I don't see why I should have to pay for it if I wasn't happy."

"You ordered the cake, I made it, and you accepted delivery. Yes, you have to pay for it." The woman probably had as much money as Donald Trump and she was going to squabble over paying for a cake that Zoey had under priced to begin with. A cake that took her twice as long to make as she anticipated because the woman insisted on a three-dimensional life-sized standing freaking poodle. No, no way.

"Hmph! I will be calling my credit card company and putting a stop to that charge."

"You do that, Mrs. Steinhoff, and I will not only see you in small claims court, I will also tell every caterer in the state what you did. You'll be blackballed. Just try and get anyone reputable to cater Isabella's birthday party next year."

"You wouldn't dare!"

"Try me." Zoey could bluff with the best of them, especially when her back was up against the wall.

There was a huff and then, "Well, I've never!"

The other line began to ring. It was really no wonder Zoey's Events was running in the red, Zoey spent all day manning the damn phone.

"I don't have any more time for you, Mrs. Steinhoff. Good day." Zoey punched the button for line two. Whoever was waiting there had to be an improvement over Mrs. Steinhoff and her precious Isabella.

Zoey put on her pleasant voice and answered. "Zoey's

Events."

"I'd like to speak with the owner, please."

Oh, boy. What now? "Speaking."

"This is County Provisions. I'm calling about an outstanding invoice."

Zoey let her head fall until it clunked against the desk, and then immediately regretted the action as the ache in her skull intensified. "I'm sure you are."

Zoey glanced at the stack of invoices on her desk. Even if she had the money in the bank account to pay them all off, which she doubted she did, when would she have the time for bookkeeping? After over two years of trying to make a go of this business and still not making a profit, she'd laid off every full-time employee she had in an attempt to turn things around. She now did all the work herself, staying late into the night seven days a week, and brought in help only on an hourly basis when absolutely necessary.

She thought she was slowly making a dent in the bills, but it was so slow, it was hard to tell for sure. How much longer would it take for this business to run in the black? Between charge cards and loans, her credit, both personal and professional, was maxed out. What she needed was one good job with a nice tidy profit to get her over the hump.

"Ms. Massey?"

"Um, yeah. Sorry. The invoice is right here on the desk in front of me. I'll cut you a check and get it out to you." She stared at the pile again, figuring the invoice probably was in there somewhere, she just didn't know exactly where.

She hung up the phone with a sigh and rose from the desk chair. Finally, for the first time in what seemed like an hour, she had a chance to leave her office—if you could call it an office. It used to be a coat closet; the rod was still there, above her head when she sat at the desk. Somehow when she dreamed of owning her own catering company, this wasn't what she'd pictured.

Sighing, she glanced at the schedule she'd hung on the wall. Custom-made penis-shaped sugar cookies. Two-dozen of them for a bachelorette party. If she weren't so tired, she might actually be amused. She'd had to visit some very interesting websites to find that particular-shaped cookie cutter. She hoped the FBI never had cause to search her internet history because after that search, there were now some pretty questionable sites on her computer's hard drive.

At least the dough for the cookies was already rolled, cut and lined up on the sheet pan like little penis shaped soldiers, waiting in the walk-in refrigerator to be baked. She flipped on the oven and was pulling them out of the fridge when the phone, once again, began to ring.

"Damn, damn, damn." Zoey flung the pan full of cookies into the oven and dashed for the phone.

"Zoey's Events."

"Hello. This is Lexi Cooper. I need to speak with someone about catering an event."

Lexi Cooper. Holy cow! *The* Lexi Cooper wanted to speak to her about an event. She tried to cover the excitement in her voice and said casually, "Sure. What's the date?"

"The week after Thanksgiving, on the Friday night. A two hour cocktail party for five hundred guests, just hors d'oeuvres."

Zoey's heart began to pound. This was it. This could be the event that paid that stack of bills on the desk. She didn't even need to check her calendar to know she was already booked on that day. A Friday night during the holidays, there was definitely something scheduled, but she'd farm that out to someone else if it meant catering a party for five hundred for Lexi Cooper.

"There's one thing, though. It's a charity event and we have to keep expenses at a bare minimum. We can't afford to pay very much. We were hoping to have you do it at your cost."

Zoey's heart sank. She was into supporting charitable causes as much as the next person, maybe more. But since she was nearly a charity case herself at this point, there was no way she could give up her already scheduled paying job during the busy holiday season in exchange for a huge undertaking that paid nothing over the cost of goods.

"I'm very sorry but I can't do it."

"But you have to do it."

Zoey smothered a laugh. The great Lexi Cooper, best selling cookbook author who apparently didn't have any financial worries, was telling her she had to do it. That was rich. No actually, it was Lexi Cooper that was rich, and she would just have to cater her own damn party.

On second thought, that was a good point. Why wasn't Lexi doing her own event?

Zoey didn't have the time or the energy to worry about Lexi's problems anymore; she had twenty-four baking penises—or was it peni—to decorate. "No, actually, I don't. Good luck finding someone, though."

Zoey hung up before she started to feel guilty and did something crazy such as accept the non-paying job. She braced two hands against the desk wearily, gathering the momentum to stand, when she smelled burning cookies and realized she hadn't set a timer.

She jumped up and heard a dull sickening thud followed by a flash of immense pain and then blackness.

Chapter 2

"What the fu…" Gordy Mullen looked up from the newspaper opened in front of him and cut off the profanity just in time.

His captain, sitting opposite him, raised a brow and glanced meaningfully at the 'cuss jar' sitting on the kitchen counter. The large glass vessel was rapidly filling with single dollar bills as the men of Engine Company 31 tried to curtail their use of profanity. Not that the sudden cleansing of their language was their idea, it had been the captain's order.

Considering Gordy would be playing Santa Claus for the kiddies in a few weeks to promote Ladder 3's nudie calendar, he figured it was probably a good idea to learn to clean up his usual potty mouth, anyway. Although so far the 'cuss jar' at the firehouse had cost him probably twenty bucks or more.

Gordy quickly veered off in another direction and completed his sentence with the word "fudge".

The captain nodded approvingly as he folded his own section of the paper and laid it on the table. "What's the problem?"

Gordy shoved the lifestyle section, which he'd been forced to read since the captain got to the sports pages first, across the table.

The captain glanced down at the photo of the smiling and happily engaged couple and frowned. "Isn't that…?"

"My ex? The woman who divorced me because she hated being married to a firefighter and then took half the house? It sure is. And look who she's marrying."

The captain squinted at the photo's caption. "Well, I'll be dam…uh, darned."

He would have smiled at the captain's near slip if he weren't so damn pissed himself. His ex was engaged to a firefighter. A proby, no less, meaning he was brand spanking new and still had the full twenty years to put in before retiring on full pension. The bitch had left Gordy when he was more than ten years in because she wouldn't wait for him to retire.

Gordy felt a quick panic over referring to his former wife—though she deserved it—as a bitch. Then he realized he had only thought the word. As far as the cuss jar went, that didn't count.

The captain pushed the paper back at him and glanced at the clock on the wall. "We're off in another thirty. You wanna hit the bar for a scotch and bitch session?"

Gordy raised a brow and glanced at the jar.

The captain noticed. "*Bitch session* doesn't count as a cuss, it is an official term."

He nodded. "Really, good to know. And no. I think I'll just head home." Gordy had realized of late, since his divorce actually, that alcohol was playing far too big a role in his off-duty hours. Besides, he was still recovering from two nights before when he'd met the guys from Ladder 3 for drinks to celebrate the release of their calendar.

He remembered the first time he'd gone out drinking with them right after the calendar photo shoot. That had been a combo tequila and bitch session, and he'd participated wholeheartedly. In fact, Gordy had been so far gone, he'd crashed at their firehouse that night. Those guys knew how to party right. That Troy was a character, delivering them all home with the pizza! It not only saved the four of them the cab fare, they had a midnight snack, too. He intended to remember that trick for future use. He bet it would work with Chinese food delivery, too.

Gordy looked up from his ponderings and found the captain observing him.

"You all right?"

Gordy nodded in response. "Fine. Happy to be rid of her. That calendar I'm in will be like a chick magnet. You wait and see."

The captain smirked. "I'm sure it will be, Mr. February. Although I still think you should have had wings and a bow and arrow. You know, like cupid."

Gordy scowled. The married guys who hadn't been allowed to model for this nude charity thing had plenty of suggestions for his humiliation. "The heart-shaped box was corny enough. Thanks, anyway."

Shrugging, the captain picked up his section of the paper again. Gordy glanced back down at the photo and then up at the clock, thinking that maybe there was a bottle of scotch in his liquor cabinet at home.

At the end of his shift, Gordy left the firehouse and starting walking for home. That was the one good thing about having to sell the house and split the profits with his ex, he now lived in an apartment walking distance from the firehouse. He tried to look at the up side of the divorce as often as possible.

Nearing the building that housed Zoey's Events, Gordy slowed his pace, trying to glance casually in the window. Here was another up side of being single again, the cute chick he could sometimes spy inside Zoey's on his walks to and from work.

Today, however, his quick glance became a stare as he stopped directly in front of the glass window.

"What the…" The storefront was filled with smoke.

At the same time his hand reached for the door handle, Gordy's eyes quickly searched the sidewalk for something to break the glass with in case the store was locked. There was a metal garbage bin. That would work if need be, but the knob turned in his hand. It was unlocked and still cool to the touch. Thank god for that. The heat within the building hadn't reached that great of a temperature yet.

He flung open the door and stepped inside. No visible flames. "Anybody in here?" No response. He didn't see anyone, but a closer look revealed to him that the smoke was coming from the back room.

He pulled his t-shirt over his nose and mouth so he could breath through it, ducked lower and headed further into the store.

In the back, a room that was obviously a professional

kitchen, black smoke billowed out of one of the ovens. Gordy flung open the oven door and got a face full of thick smoke.

"Damn." Good thing the captain wasn't there to hear him cursing.

He searched around and found a dishrag on the stainless steel counter. Grabbing it, he used it to save his hand as he pulled out a large smoldering tray and flung it onto the counter.

Confident he'd found the only cause for the smoke and that there was no actual fire, Gordy took the opportunity to turn off the oven and open the back door to let in some fresh air. As the room cleared a bit, he noticed for the first time what was on the tray. Row upon row of blackened penis cookies.

Wasn't that interesting? His cute little chef made erotic cookies for a living. Intriguing.

Speaking of the missing chef, where was she? And why was the door unlocked if the store was empty? Maybe she'd run out on an errand? Leaving the oven on with the penis cookies inside *and* the door unlocked? It didn't seem likely.

Gordy made his way back toward the front room. Should he leave the store as he found it? Wait for her to return? He was trying to decide what to do when he spied a body on the floor.

"Holy fuck." He dropped to his knees beside the motionless form. Oh, god. It was her. "Shit, shit, shit." Cursing didn't count during the discovery of bodies.

"Please don't be dead," he whispered and placed two fingers against her neck. She had a pulse, thank you god for small favors. She wasn't dead, just unconscious.

Afraid to move her, he did his best to look for injuries while barely touching her, which wasn't easy. It shouldn't be smoke inhalation; it hadn't been that thick when he'd arrived.

He had to call 9-1-1. Sure, he had first aid training, but if he couldn't find an injury, how could he treat it? Besides, he was a firefighter, not a paramedic. She needed a professional.

Gordy rose and was about to grab for the phone on the desk in the closet-sized office next to her when she moaned. He dropped back to his knees and ran one hand lightly over her forehead and hair. "It's all right. You're safe. Come on. Wake up now, sweetie."

"Ow." She groaned and raised a hand, wincing as she ran it over her hair. "My head." Then she sniffed. "Oh, no. My cookies!"

She tried to push herself up and swayed, sitting with her hand pressed to her bowed head.

"Don't try to stand up and don't worry about your cookies. I got them out, but I'm afraid if you weren't going for Cajun blackened cookies, they're a little overdone. Crispy actually. I saw the smoke from the street. That's why I came in."

She sighed and slumped against the wall, still dazed. The deep furrow in her brow told him her head still hurt like hell.

He gingerly felt until he found the egg-sized welt on her scalp. At least there was no blood. "Ooo, that's quite a lump. What happened anyway? Did you fall?"

"No, I stood." He didn't understand that until she raised a hand and pointed in the air toward the ceiling of the tiny office. Gordy looked up and noticed the clothing pole above the desk. Damn, the office *was* a closet, and she'd hit her head on the pole.

Finally convinced she wasn't going to die on him, Gordy had a moment to study the woman more intently. She was even cuter close up than he'd thought from his glimpses from the street, all light brown curly hair and green eyes, although he didn't like how large her pupils looked.

He extended his hand to her. "I'm Gordy, by the way."

"I'm Zoey." Her hand felt work-roughened in his.

"Ah, *the* Zoey of Zoey's Events." He nodded.

She laughed. "Yeah. The great chef who burnt the cookies."

Gordy smirked. "They were uh, interesting cookies."

She was so adorable, she actually blushed. "They were ordered for a bachelorette party." She groaned and covered her face with both hands. "And now they're ruined. I'm going to have to start all over." She shook her head. "I'm so tired and my skull feels like someone's hitting it with a sledge hammer. I don't know if I can do it…"

Her voice started shaking and her breath came in a sob. *Oh, boy. Here comes the tears,* Gordy thought. He slid next to her and laid one arm around her shoulders. "Shhh. It's okay. Come on, I'll take you home. Tell me where you live."

"I can't. I have to make the cookies."

He shook his head. "No. Not tonight. You probably have a concussion. I'm taking you home. Actually, I should take you to the hospital."

"No!" She looked up in panic.

"But you might have a concussion."

"I might, but I definitely do not have health insurance, so no hospital."

Gordy sighed. Even though he'd rather have a doctor's opinion, he knew enough emergency medicine to take care of her. "All right. No hospital, but I'm going to stay with you. I'll have to wake you up every two hours in case it is a concussion."

When she didn't argue, he got up and gently lifted her with him. It looked like he had actually volunteered to spend the night with a hot chick knowing there was not even the remotest chance of sex in sight. And his ex-wife had said he was immature. Ha! This was so mature he should be able to apply for AARP afterwards.

Chapter 3

"So he stayed with you, all night long."

Zoey nodded, then regretted the action. Her head still ached.

"And you have no idea who he is?" her formerly full-time, now part-time assistant chef grilled her the next morning.

"Just that his name is Gordy. That's it. I was too out of it to ask him much of anything."

"So he stays, wakes you up every two hours all night long and then just leaves?" Her right hand man looked at her in disbelief.

"No. He made me coffee and breakfast first and then left." Zoey smiled. It did seem pretty unbelievable. Maybe it had been a dream brought on by the head injury.

"Are you insane, Zoey? You could have been raped or worse, killed! And now that he's been in your apartment, he'll probably be back to rob it."

She frowned. She hadn't thought of any of that. "No, Ralph. He wasn't like that."

"Yeah, and when you met your ex-boyfriend, you told me you'd met Prince Charming. Remember that? Right before he ran up your credit card debt then split. Right before you were forced to cut my hours from full-time to practically nothing. Any of this ring a bell?"

Zoey shut her eyes against the verbal and emotional assault. What could she say? He was right.

She felt Ralph's hand on her shoulder. "I'm sorry. That was uncalled for."

"No. You're right. I'm not the best judge of character." She felt the tears begin to well in her eyes. "And I really am sorry I had to cut your hours. I had no choice. You know that, don't you?"

"I know, Zoey. You don't have to worry about me. I make in two nights at the bar what I used to make here in a week."

She laughed, bitterly. "Thanks."

Ralph smiled, his dark eyes glinting. "I'm not insinuating you don't pay well. Well, you don't, but all I'm saying is the tips are really good. I'm doing fine and I'm still available days and some nights when you need me. It's not perfect, but it will do for now. You know I want to open my own business one day. Tending bar may get me the money, but not the experience. You've taught me a lot, but I still have more to learn, so you're stuck with me."

"I'll take being stuck with you any day." She smiled weakly.

"Not to be mean, but you really do look like shit. Why don't you go back home and get some rest?"

"There's so much to do..."

"And you would have been here doing it all on your own if you didn't have a concussion and had to call me. If you can do it all alone, so can I."

Zoey sighed. "All right. Maybe just for an hour or two, but then I'm coming back. But don't forget the penis cookies for the bachelorette party."

He rolled his eyes. "Yeah, I'll remember. You're gonna owe me big for those. Hmmm. I could probably have some fun with them though. Dip the sugar cookies in white chocolate and then drizzle them with melted dark chocolate to simulate pubic hair. Maybe I'll make a few dozen extra and put them in the window for sale."

At her shocked expression he broke out laughing. "Kidding! Jeez, sense of humor much? Go. I'll be good. Boy Scout's honor." Ralph held up his fingers in the Boy Scout symbol as she started out the door, but called after her, "Don't forget to bolt your door!"

"Yes, Ralph." Getting robbed by the man that saved her, that would be just her luck. Right up there with Ralph putting erotic cookies in the window next to the display wedding cakes.

As Zoey walked the short two blocks to her apartment, she considered what Ralph had said about Gordy. At first glance, Gordy was the greatest guy she'd met in a long time. She remembered him helping her walk while supporting her with his big burly arms, the kind of arms that let you know you were really being held. She recalled reddish hair and beautiful blue eyes. He looked like he should be plowing a field somewhere in the Irish countryside a century ago. He was caring, didn't freak out at the sight of her tears and was the perfect gentleman.

Yup, that proved it. He was too good to be true, all right. The way her luck was running lately, she wouldn't be at all surprised if he turned out to be a serial killer.

Keeping that thought in mind, when she entered her apartment shortly thereafter, she took Ralph's advice and made sure she locked the deadbolt.

~

After a few days of trying to take it easy, possible concussion or not, Zoey was back in the swing of things. Ralph had helped her out immensely, but her budget didn't allow for two chefs for most of her jobs.

So here she was, alone again and staring at the schedule while feeling more than overwhelmed. The way she figured it, if she worked eighteen hours a day, she might be able to get everything done, if she didn't take the time for the long overdue bookkeeping.

Life in food service—too many things to do and not enough time to do them. This time of year was the worst of all. Happy Holidays. Ha! Whoever coined that phrase didn't work in retail or food service.

Zoey tried to force back the feeling of panic that rose in her chest when she glanced from the overfilled schedule to the stack of invoices on the desk. The bills were late anyway, what would another week hurt? Once she got through Thanksgiving weekend, she'd squeeze in some time for bill paying before the Christmas and Hanukah crunch. She wasn't able to sleep lately, anyway. Perhaps, given her insomnia, she should do the bookkeeping at night instead of lying in bed in the dark making lists of things she had left to do in her head.

She reached out a hand to turn off the desk lamp in her office and noticed her hand was trembling. Her body had been running on caffeine and adrenaline the last week, but the manifestation of this bit of physical proof was unnerving.

Blowing out a deep and she hoped calming breath, she tried to ignore the tightness in her chest. Unfortunately, it refused to be ignored. Her breath started to come in shallow gasps as her chest clenched and her heart pounded. Was this what a heart attack felt like?

Zoey grabbed the phone. She couldn't call 9-1-1, they would take her to the hospital and she'd canceled the company's health insurance policy months ago to save money. Ralph. He'd know what to do. Not knowing if he'd be at home or at the bar, she dialed his cell phone number. She was shaking so badly and breathing so hard, she misdialed twice.

She was starting to panic enough to reconsider calling an ambulance. No, she'd try to get Ralph one more time. Her clumsy fingers pushed the hopefully correct sequence of buttons when black spots suddenly started to appear in front of her vision.

This is it, she thought. *I'm going to die, here, all alone.* Then she glanced up and through the front window saw Gordy out on the sidewalk. Phone forgotten, she stood, took once step toward the door, and collapsed to her knees.

Even though she didn't remember hearing the door open, in spite of the bells hung there, he was suddenly beside her. Strong hands held her face and forced her to look up. She gasped, still trying to catch her breath, and clutched at his forearms.

"Heart attack?" she managed to say.

Gordy shook his head. "No. I think you're just hyperventilating."

She was aware that he left her, and when he returned, he had a paper bag in his hand.

"Breath into this slowly. There's too much oxygen in

your system. You're going to be fine. I promise. Just stay calm."

Zoey did as he asked, not that she had much choice in the matter. He placed the bag over her nose and mouth and held it there with one massive hand while firmly cupping the back of her head with the other.

When she began to enjoy the feel of his hand in her hair and to consider that this guy had touched her more during this past week than any other man had in months, she decided she must be feeling better.

Her breathing slowed enough that he finally took the bag away from her face. "How do you feel?"

"Better." She pursed her lips, feeling embarrassed. "You seem to always be saving me. Thank you."

He smiled broadly at her. "It's my job and my pleasure." His fingers massaged the back of her neck gently. It was so nice to have someone taking care of her after having to take care of everything all by herself for so long. She couldn't help it, she leaned into him and dropped her head against his broad chest.

"I was so scared."

His strong arms enveloped her and she felt him kiss the top of her head. "I know. It's all right now."

She didn't know how long he held her like that, but the next thing she was aware of was the jangling sound of the door opening again.

Looking up, she saw Ralph standing in the doorway with a strange look on his face. "Zoey? Are you okay?"

She nodded. "Better now. Thanks."

Ralph was breathing heavily as if he'd run there. "You called my cell phone and then hung up. I tried calling back and the phone was busy."

She glanced at the desk and noticed the receiver dangling off the edge of the desk, suspended only by the phone cord.

Bracing against Gordy for support, Zoey stood and replaced the receiver in the cradle. "Sorry, Ralph."

"What exactly happened?" Ralph's eyes were darting back and forth between her and Gordy suspiciously.

Zoey realized Ralph probably assumed she had been attacked. She wouldn't doubt if he had run all the way there to save her. He was a good kid. "I think I hyperventilated, but Gordy arrived just in time to help me."

"Looked like a panic attack to me." Gordy pushed her down into the desk chair and laid the back of his hand against her brow while looking closely at her eyes.

Ralph looked more angry than concerned now. "A panic attack? Damn it, Zoey. When are you going to face that you can't run this place on your own? After you finally work yourself to death? That's it. I don't care if you can't afford to pay me. I'll work for free until you start making enough money. You need to start taking better care of yourself."

Gordy looked down at her. "He's right, Zoey. I went to a funeral for a friend of mine recently. He went to sleep one night and didn't wake up in the morning. He was forty years old."

"See!" Ralph piped in.

Zoey looked up and saw Ralph narrow his eyes at Gordy. "Why do you look so familiar?"

Gordy finally looked away from her long enough to glance at Ralph. "You tend bar at *The Lamplight*?"

Ralph nodded and she saw realization strike in his eyes. "You've been in there with the guys from the firehouse."

Gordy nodded. "Yup. Gordy Mullen."

Ralph grinned. "So *you're* Zoey's Gordy, huh?"

Zoey had sat silently and calmly watched the testosterone face-off right up until the time Ralph called Gordy 'hers', then all semblance of calm faded.

Heart pounding again, she glanced up quickly at Gordy's face and noticed him looking too happy. She frowned. "He means you're the guy who found me the other night. That's all."

Gordy raised a brow. "Oh."

"Well, yeah. I mean, I had to tell him all about it because

I needed him to cover for me. You know, because of the concussion."

Gordy nodded, still grinning. She couldn't even imagine what he thought she'd told Ralph about him.

"Well, I really have to get back to work. Thanks again." She would have loved to physically lead both of the men out the door so she could be alone with her embarrassment but that would have looked worse.

She noticed Gordy shaking his head. "No."

Zoey frowned. "What do you mean no?"

"Take him up on his offer. You need a break or the next attack might not be just a panic attack."

"Fine. I'll take an hour off and, I don't know, go eat breakfast or something."

"Zoey! You haven't eaten yet?" Ralph pointedly looked at the wall clock, which was reading closer to lunchtime than breakfast.

Gordy scowled. "Yes, you should take an hour to eat, but I'm talking about a real break. Like a week off."

"I agree. I looked over the schedule yesterday. I could handle things for a week." Ralph stepped closer to Gordy. A show of male solidarity, she supposed.

Great. This was what she needed, both men ganging up on her.

"A week!" Even just the thought of it made her stomach clutch in panic. "I can't do that." Next week was Thanksgiving, she was busy.

The sudden ringing of the phone was for once a welcome sound. Saved by the bell. "I have to get that."

She watched them both stand right where they were, rigid and unmoving. With a sigh, she reached for the receiver. "Zoey's Events."

"Ms. Massey?"

Please, don't let it be another creditor. She didn't think her heart could take it at the moment. "Speaking."

"This is John White, your aunt's attorney. I'm afraid I have some bad news for you."

Chapter 4

Gordy sat opposite Zoey in the coffee shop. Her face was still pale, her breathing shallow. The phone call had been a shock for her. And still, it had taken both him and Ralph the bartender/part-time chef to convince her she needed to leave her storefront. Even a death in the family couldn't crack this woman's dedication.

"I just can't believe it. She was my father's younger sister. She is…I mean she *was* less than twenty years older than me. And now she's gone."

Gordy reached out and squeezed her hand. "Have you spoken to your father yet?"

She looked at him with a glazed expression and then shook her head. She laughed, tears glistening in her eyes. "I keep forgetting I barely know you. My parents are both dead. Car crash a few years ago. Aunt Zoe was the only relative I had left."

Gordy raised a brow. "You were named for her."

Zoey nodded. "She never married or had kids, so I was pretty special to her. She's the one who taught me to cook. She had a little business baking cookies and cakes in a small town in Connecticut. I loved visiting her old farmhouse when I was a kid. She used to have chickens for fresh eggs for her baking…"

Gordy watched the tears fill her eyes and spill over. He handed her a paper napkin from the dispenser.

She took it and wiped her eyes. "I haven't been to visit her in the two years since I opened this business. I should have taken the time…now it's too late."

Reaching into his pocket, Gordy pulled out cash for the bill, slid it under his mug and stood. "Come on. I'm taking you home."

She rose without an argument and let him lead her to her apartment. When they reached her door, she turned. "I'm going to have to drive out to Connecticut. The lawyer says I need to be there for the reading of the will. She's got close girlfriends who are making the arrangements, but I feel like I need to be there to help. I'm the only blood relative." Her voice cracked on the word 'arrangements', a lovely euphemism but they both new what she meant.

He reached out and laid a hand on her shoulder. "If there is anything I can do..."

She grabbed his hand and held it tightly. "There is. You can come inside."

"Okay." Poor thing needed a shoulder to cry on. It had been a rough week for her with the concussion, thinking she was having a heart attack and now the death of her closest relative. If he could help her just by being there, it was the least he could do.

As Zoey unlocked the door and led him inside, he spared a brief regret that they couldn't have met at a happy time in her life. A time when her business wasn't floundering and she wasn't on the verge of a nervous breakdown. He liked her, more than he wanted to admit at the moment because as far as timing went, this, right now, was just plain bad. No way around it.

He didn't have any more time to think about it though, because the moment he shut the door behind them, her arms were around his neck and her mouth covered his.

Raw instinct had him wrapping his hands around her waist and kissing her back until he finally realized what he was doing and pulled back from her. "Zoey."

"I want you, Gordy."

He shook his head. "No, sweetie. You only think you do. I've seen it happen before. Women will suddenly think they are in love with a fireman or a paramedic just because he saved her."

"That's not it. I need you, Gordy. I need to feel alive and forget about all the bad stuff for a little while."

She reached up for his mouth again, looking so sad and vulnerable and all right, sexy, too, that he nearly gave in and kissed her. Dammit, he couldn't do it. She was a victim and he couldn't take advantage of her when she was in this state.

He physically held her about a foot away from him but it was one of the harder things he'd ever done. "Zoey. You've been through a lot lately. You're in shock and don't know what you're doing."

Her eyes filled with tears. "You can just say it. It's all right. You don't find me attractive. I understand." She pulled away from him and went to stand on the other side of the room. He watched her shoulders shake as she cried silently and stared out the window.

Without thinking he crossed the room in a few long strides, spun her around by the shoulders and kissed her fiercely. Her breath caught in her throat as he bent her backwards over his arm, plunging his tongue into her warm, welcoming mouth. He tangled his one hand in her hair, angled her head and kissed her deeper.

Barely lifting his head from hers, he spoke close to her mouth. "Don't you ever think that I don't find you attractive. I do. And when this hell you're in has passed, if you still want me in your bed—and god, I hope you do—I swear to you I will come running, but not now, sweetie. Not now."

She placed two trembling hands on his face and planted a soft and very brief tear-filled kiss on his lips. Leaning her forehead against his, she nodded.

With a deep breath, Gordy held her tighter to him, knowing this was as close as he'd be getting to her for the near future and it had been his own choice. When exactly had he become such a saint? More importantly, he wondered how much longer his newfound piousness was going to last, because he really liked the feel of Zoey in his arms.

He rubbed her back. "Come on. I'll make you some tea while you start packing for Connecticut. Make sure you bring warm clothes, a cold front is supposed to be moving in."

She pulled away and nodded, walking away from him toward her bedroom. He watched her go and pictured her naked in his arms as they snuggled under a down comforter during a snowstorm...

He shook his head to clear the image and headed for the kitchen. Damn conscience. More trouble than it was worth, if you asked him.

So instead of making love to a beautiful woman, Gordy made tea. Then he helped Zoey drag her suitcase out of the storage room in the basement of her apartment building and watched her pack to go far away from him, for how long he didn't know.

He was thinking that he truly was a stupid man as he hoisted the giant bag she'd packed into the back of her car. He didn't like that she'd packed so much, didn't like it one little bit. It only meant that she was planning on staying away for a long time and that thought, in light of his recent self-denial, just plain sucked.

Gordy absently noted that Zoey's station wagon smelled a bit like garlic as he put the suitcase in. Of course, she must use the car for food deliveries. It was just sad that she couldn't get away from her work even in her car. Hopefully she was so used to the way her car smelled that it wouldn't remind her during the entire drive of her business problems. She didn't need anything else to worry her at the moment and that, he reminded himself, included starting a physical relationship with him right now.

He slammed the back closed and walked around the car. Zoey was standing next to the open driver's side door. He stepped closer and ran his hands up and down the arms of Zoey's coat. "Drive safely, okay? Don't go too fast."

She nodded and blushed a bit. "Yes, sir."

Gordy smiled. "Sorry, I'm a worrier."

"Don't apologize. It's nice to be worried about once in a while."

He leaned down, intending to only give her a casual kiss goodbye. It didn't exactly turn out that way. The kiss they shared was anything but casual and left him breathless. He was ready to throw away his earlier convictions about waiting for her to get back and settled before letting anything happen between them.

Gordy finally broke away. "All right, then. You have my cell phone number in case you need anything?"

She nodded, looking a little flushed from the kiss herself.

"Good. And I have yours, too. So…" The babbling took his mind off of wanting to drag her back up to the apartment, but just barely.

"So…" she repeated.

He ran a thumb over her lower lip, and then dropped his hand reluctantly and took one step back. "Bye."

"Bye." She got behind the wheel and he closed the door for her.

As he watched her drive away he added, "Don't be gone too long." He waited for the car to be completely out of view before he turned and made his way to the firehouse. He was going to be early for a long, frustrating shift filled with regret and thoughts of Zoey, but what the hell else did he have to do?

~

A few days later, Gordy stepped into The Lamplight. Determined, he went directly to the bar, but it wasn't a drink he was after, it was Zoey. She'd be back eventually, hopefully in a few days or less, and when she returned, he vowed to relieve her of some of the pressure she was under. It wasn't totally selfless. The sooner Zoey got her life on track, the sooner Gordy could be a bigger, more intimate part of it.

Luck was on his side. Ralph stood behind the bar wiping glasses. The young chef was probably his best bet for gathering information that could help Zoey. Ralph greeted him the moment he stepped through the door. "Gordy! What can I get for you?"

He needed his wits about him so he ordered something non-alcoholic. "Uh, plain cranberry juice, thanks."

Ralph nodded and set about making his drink while Gordy took the opportunity for some fact finding. "How are things going over at Zoey's?"

Putting the tall glass on the bar in front of Gordy, Ralph shook his head. "That woman, I swear. She has a schedule of events put together for this week that no single human being could possibly handle alone and she was intending on doing it all by herself."

"Hence the panic attack," Gordy supplied.

"Exactly!" Ralph agreed.

"Then how are you handling it while keeping your shift here?"

"I called in a favor and got my roommate, who graduated from cooking school with me, to help with everything that could be prepped and cooked in advance. Then I called the school and got myself two interns for rock bottom wage. They need a lot of supervision, but they're cheap."

"Why didn't Zoey do that herself?"

"Because she has a martyr complex? And she says she doesn't have the money in the company to pay any extra hands."

"But she's going to have to pay the two you got."

Ralph shook his head. "I have a plan for that. She's got too much work for one person, but not enough business to support two or three chefs. However, I figure with taking on the extra help I can also take on more jobs, therefore making more money, which will pay for the extra help. It's the holidays, man. Her phone is ringing off the hook with business. I can only guess she was turning jobs down because she couldn't do it all alone."

Gordy nodded. Ralph's plan sounded good in theory, not that he knew anything about the catering business. Gordy could cook some killer hot wings, though. The guys at the firehouse loved them.

He frowned. "It just seems odd Zoey didn't realize that more help and more jobs would make more money herself."

"I gotta tell you, man. Zoey's creative and hardworking, she's got vision and talent that you can't learn in school, but she's got no head for business. I finally went through the pile of invoices on her desk. She's got no filing system. She was paying friggin' twenty-one percent interest on her credit card balance! I couldn't stand it anymore. I spent last night organizing it all. She left me a stack of signed checks so I paid off what I could and I moved her outstanding credit card balance to her other card, which has zero percent interest on transfers for six months. With the money she saves on that alone, she will be able to pay the rent for the month."

Gordy considered the revelation carefully. "Sounds like you've got a pretty good head for business yourself, Ralph."

Ralph nodded. "I got a two year degree in business before I went to cooking school. I wanna open my own place and I need to be able to handle all aspects myself. Problem is, I don't have what Zoey has. I can cook all right, but the whole ability to design an event, right down to the details, nope, she's the man when it comes to that stuff."

A plan began to form. "You know, Ralph, it sounds to me like if we put you with your business sense and Zoey with her creativity together, we'd have the perfect caterer."

Ralph nodded and laughed. "Yeah. You're right." Gordy waited a beat as Ralph absorbed what he'd hinted at. "You're suggesting a partnership?"

Gordy nodded. "That's exactly what I'm suggesting."

Ralph looked at him a bit closer. "And what exactly are *you* after when it comes to Zoey?"

Gordy smiled. "A different kind of partnership between Zoey and I."

"Zoey means a lot to me." Ralph's voice was low with warning.

"In what way?" Gordy wasn't too worried. Zoey wouldn't have been inviting him to her bed if she felt anything romantic for her assistant chef. Of that, Gordy was sure. A crush on Ralph's part would complicate things, though, and lose him Ralph as an ally in Gordy's quest to relieve Zoey of some of the pressure in her life so he could crawl into her bed with a clear conscience.

Leaning across the bar, Ralph hissed, "In the 'she's my friend and if you hurt her I'll hurt you' kind of way."

Gordy smiled at the young man's devotion. "Then we have no problem between us. We both want the same things for Zoey—a successful business that doesn't kill her in the process."

"And leaves her enough free time for a serious boyfriend, perhaps?" Ralph suggested.

Gordy nodded. "That would be very nice."

The cell phone clipped to Ralph's belt began emitting a lively tune. He held up a finger to Gordy. "Hold that thought."

While Ralph answered the call, Gordy sipped at his cranberry juice. Idle fantasies of a relaxed, carefree, no longer overworked Zoey filled his head, until Ralph walked closer to him and said a bit louder, "Don't worry about a thing, Zoey. I've got it handled... What do you mean, how? You were planning on doing it all yourself, why don't you think I can handle it myself. And on top of getting all the jobs done on time, I also organized your invoices, paid the overdue ones and created an expense and income spreadsheet in your computer... Apology accepted." Ralph grinned at Gordy. "Hey, when you get back, I want to talk to you about something... No, it can wait until you get back."

Ralph hesitated and opened his eyes wide. "Have I seen Gordy around lately? Um..."

Gordy nodded enthusiastically and held out his hand for the phone.

Ralph said, "You're in luck, Zoe. He just walked into the bar. Here he is."

Gordy grabbed the phone just as he heard Zoey protesting, "No, Ralph. That's okay. Don't..."

He stopped her before she said something he didn't want to hear. "Hi, it's me."

"Oh, hi. I just didn't want him to bother you in case you didn't want to talk to me." She sounded sincere...and insecure.

He could easily alleviate her insecurity. "I've thought about nothing except calling you since you left."

"Then why didn't you call?"

"I wanted to give you some space to deal with your aunt's death and things there in Connecticut. And I was on shift at the firehouse and frustrated enough at knowing I couldn't see you."

"Do you want to see me?" Damn, she sounded sexy.

He found himself cradling Ralph's phone a little closer to his ear. "Oh, yeah." Nothing he wanted more.

"Do you want to drive out today?" She sounded very flirtatious.

His resolve was immediately lost as his heart skipped a beat. "You want me to?"

"Mmm, hmm."

He signaled to Ralph for a pen and a cocktail napkin. "Give me the directions."

Chapter 5

Zoey hung up the phone and looked at the group of women that surrounded her in the old farmhouse kitchen. This was the kitchen where her Aunt Zoe had taught her to cook those many years ago. The place where her aunt's nearest and dearest three friends had congregated so often. Over the years, they'd all shared food, wine, laughter and tears, good times and bad in this kitchen. Now, they dealt with their grief over her loss here, too.

Having her aunt's closest friends there with her during this period of mourning both helped and hurt a little at the same time. There were strong memories in that house, for all of them.

The first few days after Zoey's arrival, the plans and arrangements for the funeral and settling the estate had consumed all of them completely. But with both the funeral and the meeting with the lawyer done, it seemed her aunt's friends took on a new project—Zoey.

It was probably their way of getting over her Aunt Zoe's death themselves, but it suddenly seemed that Zoey's love life was their pet project and main immediate concern. That she'd made the mistake of mentioning Gordy to the three matchmakers only added fuel to the fire. A possible love connection for Zoey was like blood in the water and these women were the sharks. They bit into the task of securing her a man single-mindedly.

"Is he coming?" Maizie asked excitedly.

Zoey nodded, wishing she could share Maizie's excitement. Right now she was too overwhelmed with guilt. She was inviting a man to spend the night less than a week after her aunt's death, and she had a feeling they would probably end up doing some very wicked things in her aunt's house. There was also the feeling of panic residing low in her belly with the thought of seeing—and doing more—with Gordy.

"Good. Now, we have a ton of things to do." Like a

general staging an all-out military attack, Maizie outlined the plan. "I'm going to start a pot of good old Irish stew. It sounds like your Gordy would like that, and it will hold on the stove in case you two get distracted for a few hours, if you know what I mean."

Zoey blushed at the older woman's insinuation, but didn't argue.

"Rosemary. You straighten up around here from this drunken cry fest we've been having since Zoey arrived," Maizie barked. "Can't have the man seeing the house a shambles."

Rosemary nodded like an obedient soldier. Zoey took a glance around at the discarded tissues, coffee mugs and wine bottles littering the table and countertop and had to agree.

Maizie forged boldly onward. "Louise. You make a fire in the fireplace. Then find every candle in this house and put them all around the living room."

Louise nodded. "Good plan. A woman's looks always benefit from candlelight. Even if she is as young and beautiful as our Zoey, here."

"Thanks, Aunt Louise." Zoey smiled at her aunt's friends, all of whom she'd grown up calling 'aunt' even though they were not blood relatives. 'Honorary aunts' they called themselves and they had always been an important part of her life and Aunt Zoe's too. They were there for Aunt Zoe when she discovered, just two months ago, that she had lung cancer. Never smoked a day in her life but it took her anyway and in less time than anyone could have imagined.

The thought and the sadness must have shown on Zoey's face because all three women were suddenly surrounding her. "She did what she thought was right, Zoey. She knew you were busy with the new business and she knew you would abandon everything to come and hold her hand for however long it took," Rosemary explained gently.

"Well, I never agreed with it. Swearing us all to secrecy so we couldn't even tell you. She should have considered how you would feel, Zoey." Maizie shook her head.

"She thought she had more time, Maizie. We all did. Even the doctors were shocked. She was going to tell you right after the holidays, Zoey," Louise explained. "She just went to bed one night and didn't wake up."

Renewed tears in her eyes, Zoey nodded, remembering Gordy had told her nearly the same thing about his friend who'd died without any warning. "I guess we all think we'll have more time."

It had been that realization that made Zoey take that frightful step and invite Gordy to the farmhouse. She'd thrown herself at him once already in her apartment, only to be rebuked. It was really putting her feelings out on the line again to take this latest action, but the aunts wouldn't have had it any other way.

All four wiped their eyes again. Maizie took another slug of wine and straightened her spine. "Okay. Enough pity. This is not what Zoe would have wanted."

They all nodded their agreement, Rosemary with a big added sniff.

Maizie clapped her hands to rally the troops. "All right, ladies. No time to waste. We don't have all day. Zoey's Gordy will be here in just a few hours. Chop, chop! You have your assignments."

Zoey raised her hand. "Um, I didn't get an assignment."

Maizie swung toward her. "Your job is to get yourself ready for Gordy. Go take a bubble bath, put on some perfume and your prettiest outfit. Something easy to get out of."

Zoey blushed again. These women, all of an indiscernible age ranging somewhere between fifty and sixty, were not shy when it came to sex.

Maizie shoved another glass of wine in her hand and shooed her out of the kitchen saying, "Don't forget to wash all the important parts real well."

Zoey seriously considered drowning herself in the tub.

~

Gordy drove the distance to Connecticut in record time.

The roads were dry and he was anxious to get there. Thankfully, he was also lucky and didn't get caught in a speed trap. He stopped during the trip only long enough to pick up a bunch of flowers for Zoey.

His overnight bag was in the back seat. He supposed it was making a big assumption to bring an overnight bag, although Zoey wouldn't have invited him to drive this far without assuming he'd stay overnight. Besides, he'd sleep on the couch if she wasn't ready for anything more.

Gordy considered. Would she be ready? She'd only had a few days to get over her aunt's death and get her affairs in order with the lawyer. Come to think of it, was he ready?

Oh, he knew his body was more than ready to sink into Zoey, but his mind knew making love to Zoey wouldn't be just a one-night stand. He wanted to begin their relationship on the right foot. Just the thought of that surprised him a bit. He hadn't even considered a serious relationship since his divorce. Why was he jumping through hoops to insure one with Zoey now?

He'd originally agreed to pose in the fireman calendar thinking it would yield him a disposable bounty of quick sex with anonymous women. That had somehow seemed very appealing to him at the time. It wasn't so tempting anymore. Being with Zoey would completely negate that original plan and that thought didn't disappoint him one bit.

The conversation he'd had with the Ladder 3 guys a few months ago flashed through his mind. How Troy and Antonio had lectured Scotty that he'd know when he found 'the one'. Was Zoey the one for him? Who knew? He'd thought his ex was the one at the time, too. Maybe he should wait.

He sighed and brought his mind back to the road. As he neared the small Connecticut town where Zoey was, his heart started to beat a bit faster. He had two days before he had to be back for a shift at the firehouse. It wasn't a lot of time with her, but it might be enough to figure things out. If it wasn't, there was always later, when she returned to the city.

The town was so small, Gordy blinked and nearly missed it. Before he knew it, he was pulling slowly down a dead end road that he hoped led to Zoey. He spied the mailbox with the number she'd given him and steeled his nerves. As anxious as he'd been to arrive, he was still nervous about actually being there.

A large square boat of a car pulled out of the driveway and three faces within turned his way. Gordy glanced down at the cocktail napkin that contained the directions and confirmed that this was indeed the house number she'd given him. Maybe it was a shared drive or something. Of course, they could be mourners come to pay their respects.

That thought made Gordy reconsider once again letting anything happen with Zoey during this visit. She was still in mourning for a beloved aunt, the only relative she had left. She was truly an orphan now. Gordy had an overwhelmingly huge family. He could barely comprehend the thought of being alone in the world, but he knew he couldn't take advantage of Zoey's fears of being by herself.

But what if she wanted him to be with her as part of the healing process? He sighed, confused and frustrated. Relationships were just plain complicated. No wonder the idea of casual sex had seemed so appealing to him. Now that it was too late, he realized he was hooked on Zoey. Casual was not an option anymore.

He would just let her lead them. Whichever way she wanted to take tonight, whether it was platonic or passionate, he would follow.

With that resolution made, he drove down the long gravel driveway and parked near the house. Getting out of the car, he smelled snow in the air. It didn't often snow in November, but it sure felt like a storm was coming. It would be just his luck to get snowed in with Zoey after he'd resolved not to sleep with her if she didn't want that.

Why was his life so complicated? He considered that as he knocked on the door. He stood with the flowers in hand as he waited for her to answer. The overnight bag would stay in the car until he assessed the atmosphere.

She opened the door and he began assessing immediately. Her warm smile greeted him along with the scent of stew cooking. Closing the door against the cold, she'd pulled him into a candlelit room where a fire roared in the hearth and music played softly. A mound of pillows and a throw were on the floor in front of the fire and a bottle of wine and two glasses sat on the table. The scene screamed seduction.

Gordy pulled his gaze back to Zoey. He remembered the flowers. "Here, these are for you."

She took them and reached up to kiss his mouth softly. "Thank you. They're beautiful."

He took in her appearance. She was dressed in something that looked like a very dressy, clingy sweat suit. He reached out a hand and touched the incredibly soft fabric. Of course, as nice as the outfit felt, he still couldn't help picturing peeling it off of her. "This is nice. You look good."

She smiled. "Thank you. I'm going to go put these in water and stir the stew. Are you hungry?"

"Um, sure. If you are." He hung his coat on the hooks behind the front door and followed her into the kitchen. Immediately he got a feeling of why she loved visiting her aunt as a child. The room, the whole house really, radiated warmth.

Zoey grabbed a pitcher off one of the open kitchen shelves and filled it with water and flowers. She gave the stew one quick stir and looked back at him. "Maybe we can have a glass of wine by the fire first and then eat."

Gordy listened to her words, which were plain and straightforward enough, but the meaning and emotion behind the words caught him by surprise. Was he mistaken, or was she was coming on to him? He swallowed hard. "Sounds good."

She grabbed his hand and led him back to the other room. After she'd poured them both a glass of wine, the way she arranged herself seductively on the pillow-strewn floor made his breath catch in his throat.

He hesitated and watched the doubt replace the confidence on her face. Quickly sitting next to her, he rubbed her neck and asked, "How are you doing?"

Bringing up her aunt's death and her grief was probably the surest way to kill any thoughts of romance but he needed to know.

"It's been tough, but my aunt's friends have helped so much." Zoey went on to explain her aunt's diagnosis and the speed with which the cancer took her. But instead of tears, Gordy saw a new determination in Zoey.

"It sounds like this trip has been good for you so far."

She nodded, sat up and put her glass on the floor. "It has, in lots of ways. It's taught me that life is short and I shouldn't put off doing what I want. Like this cashmere sweat suit, Aunt Zoe gave it to me last year for Christmas. I've worn it once. I was always afraid to wear it because it seemed too nice. I was saving it, for what I don't know. I'm through doing that."

Gordy smiled. "Good for you, Zoey."

She dropped her eyes briefly and then raised them to look at him again. "You told me in my apartment to never doubt that you wanted me, but that I needed to get myself straightened out first."

Gordy drew in a deep breath and nodded.

"I never felt clearer about what I want in my life than I do right now."

"What do you want, Zoey?"

"I want you." She dropped her eyes again.

Relieved, Gordy let out the breath he'd been holding, put his own glass on the floor and raised her chin with one finger. "I'm very glad to hear that." He smiled. "And doubly glad I have two days off and my bag packed in the car. If that's all right."

She nodded. "Yeah. It's all very right."

He swallowed and leaned in until their lips touched and

then pulled back. "You sure?"

"Yes."

"Good."

The cashmere outfit didn't last long. Neither did his jeans and shirt. Between the heat of the fire and the warmth of Zoey's body, he was bathed in perspiration, but he didn't care. Real sex, particularly really good sex, was a messy, often sweaty business. It was also a good excuse to take a shower together after. A really long steamy shower for two that only ended when the hot water ran out.

By the time they got to eating the stew, much, much later that night, the meat was so tender it fell off the fork.

Chapter 6

Zoey opened her eyes late the next morning as the November sun streamed through the bedroom curtains. She sighed and stretched, feeling better than she had in years. Probably because she'd had the best sleep she'd had in a long time following the best sex she'd had ever.

Speaking of that…she noticed the empty spot in the bed next to her where Gordy should have been. Then she smelled coffee and bacon and smiled. He was cooking her breakfast. Wasn't that a nice change, someone cooking for her instead of the other way around?

Snuggling lower under the covers, she wondered if she should go downstairs and join him in the kitchen or if he would bring her breakfast in bed. The fact that she was too warm and happy to consider moving at the moment made the decision for her. Before very long, Gordy appeared, wearing just sweatpants and carrying a tray.

She smiled and sat up against the headboard. "Good morning."

"Good morning yourself. You were sleeping so cute, I thought I'd sneak down and make myself at home in the kitchen. I hope that's okay."

"You can cook for me anytime you want. No problem."

He laughed. "You better taste it first before you start making offers like that."

She dug hungrily into the soft-boiled egg and the pile of bacon. When it was half gone, she glanced up at him guiltily. "Aren't you going to eat?"

He grinned. "I nibbled while I was cooking. You just eat. Don't worry about me. I'll join you when you get to the dessert."

She noticed for the first time a bowl of whipped cream and strawberries on the tray.

"Yummy."

"Oh, it will be." Gordy ran a hand suggestively down her arm and waggled his eyebrows. Zoey's eyes opened wide.

Gordy's hearty laugh filled the small room. "That is not the face of a woman who makes penis cookies for a living. Don't tell me you've never done more with whipped cream than just cook."

She swallowed hard and shook her head. Her sexual experience up to this point had been pretty much missionary position in a bed. In fact, she'd thought last night's escapade on the floor in front of the fire followed by a shower with Gordy had been extremely wild.

She felt her face grow warm. Gordy shook his head and leaned over her. "How can anyone be so cute and innocent looking and so damn sexy at the same time?"

He kissed her mouth and then got up. Putting the tray on the dresser by the window, he returned to the bed with the bowl of strawberries and whipped cream. He held one cream covered strawberry in the air. "Open up."

She obediently opened her mouth and accepted the berry. This wasn't too bad, actually. She could handle being fed strawberries and cream in bed.

He put the bowl on the table next to the bed, leaned over and covered her lips with his, his tongue sweeping inside her mouth. "Mmm, you taste good." His hands made their way under her nightshirt, pushing it up her body. "I wanna taste all of you."

The shirt was suddenly off, lying on the floor next to the bed. She felt the cool morning air make her nipples pucker. If the air hadn't had done it, the cold whipped cream Gordy scooped up with one finger and dabbed on the tip of each breast would have.

Her breath caught in her throat as he lowered his head and ate the cream right from her body, first from one nipple, then from the other. He lapped it right up like a cat, and then scraped his teeth gently against the tip of each breast. She shuddered.

He looked up and smiled. "You really have never done anything like this before have you?"

She shook her head.

144

He grinned. "Good. I like being the one to show you new things." He slid lower down her naked body, trailing kisses until he reached the apex of her thighs. He spread her legs and reached again for the cream.

The sound of her sharp intake of breath filled the room. "Gordy!"

He glanced up and mimicked her. "Zoey!"

"You're not going to put it down there, are you?"

He grinned. "Just watch me."

She leaned her head back against the bed. Not thinking she could watch, she squeezed her eyes shut as she felt him spread whipped cream on her and in her. The feel of it made her shiver until the heat of his tongue replaced the cold. She couldn't argue, it felt amazing as his mouth made short work of the cream and of her insecurities.

She raised her hips off the bed, seeking more when, even after the cream was gone, he continued working her and filling her with tongue and fingers until her body began to shudder. She'd thought he had been a master the night before, but he was even more incredible that morning. She came with a powerful orgasm that elicited a moan even from Gordy.

He finally pulled himself up the bed and collapsed on the pillow next to her. "Aren't you glad now that you let me corrupt you?"

She nodded. "But I don't think you're done yet." Reaching for the bowl herself she said, "Drop the sweats."

Now it was his turn to look shocked, but only for a second. "Whatever you say."

With Gordy naked except for some strategically placed whipped cream, Zoey soon taught him that she could be a very quick learner. Being a chef, after all, it was only proper that she experience all the uses for whipped cream personally.

~

"She left me the house and all her money," Zoey announced much later when they were still lounging in bed.

Gordy stroked her face. "That must mean a lot to you. I know you have fond memories of your aunt in this house."

Zoey nodded and hesitated a moment. "I think I'm staying."

As she raised her head from his chest, he looked down and frowned. "You mean commute? That's a long drive."

She shook her head and sat up to look him in the eye. "Just being here, even for a few days, I feel...I don't know...at peace." She sighed. "And every time I think about going back to work, my chest gets tight and I feel like I need to throw up."

Gordy's arm around her shoulders tightened. "But what would you do here? For work, I mean. Did your aunt leave you enough money that you could totally retire?"

She shook her head and laughed. "No. Not even close. There's enough to run the house for a few years, but that's it. I guess I'd reopen her business. Small catering jobs, specialized cookies and cakes." She shrugged. "I don't know. I haven't really thought it through."

"Zoey, you have to be the one to make this decision, but I have one suggestion. Ralph is handling your company just fine for now. You've been through a lot of changes lately. I suggest you take a bit of time to just breathe. Don't rush into any decisions yet. Take time off, live here for a while and see how you like it. But don't do anything final like close your business or give up your apartment. Not yet."

Quietly considering for a moment, Zoey finally nodded. "Okay." Then she frowned. "Ralph is really handling it all alone with no problem? Maybe that proves I should close the business."

"No, sweetie. It doesn't. It proves that he has a chef roommate who owed him a favor and they are both working their butts off because you had more work than one person could possibly handle."

She smiled. "Really?"

He held up one hand. "Honest."

"That makes me feel a little better."

146

"Good, it should. You know, Ralph has a good business head on his shoulders. He'd make a great partner for someone who loves the creative side and hates paperwork and bookkeeping."

Okay, so that wasn't very subtle. It was clear what Gordy was getting at. She couldn't run her business alone any longer. If she didn't close it up and move to Connecticut permanently, she would have to make plans to take on Ralph or someone else as a partner for Zoey's Events.

"Was that supposed to be a hint?" She raised a brow at him.

"Maybe."

She didn't want to think about it any more now. "Well, here is a hint for you." She ran one fingernail down the dusting of reddish blond hair that covered his chest.

He smiled. "I wasn't on the honor roll or anything at school, but I can take a hint."

Before Zoey knew it, she was experiencing yet another position with Gordy that definitely had nothing to do with missionaries.

Chapter 7

He'd done his job well, too well. Gordy had wanted Zoey to learn to relax, but now there was a chance he was going to lose her to some tiny town in friggin' nowhere Connecticut. The thought of walking past her store and not seeing her inside everyday made him a little sick to his stomach.

Of course she should keep the house that she loved, but as a vacation house, not to live in fulltime after she closed her business. He'd hinted, not so subtlety, that he thought she should take Ralph on as a partner, but that was all he could do. The decision was hers to make.

He started calculating how much time he would have to spend on the road, driving back and forth to see her every two days when he was off. That was of course if she didn't decide that he was part of her old life in the city and dump him right along with her business. Damn, he hated the feeling of having no control.

He let out a long frustrated breath.

"What's up with you?"

Gordy glanced up at his new friend Scott, guiltily realizing he hadn't been holding up his portion of the assembly line. Somehow, he'd gotten roped into helping cook for the damn fundraising cocktail party. He stood now, slicing green peppers for the crudite, which he just recently learned meant fresh vegetables for dip.

As distracted as he was, he really shouldn't have a sharp implement in his hand. He sighed and answered Scott's question. "Woman trouble."

Scott laughed. "I know what you mean."

Gordy raised a brow. "You, too?"

Scott shrugged. "Knock wood things are fine at the moment, that is as long as the catering thing tomorrow goes smoothly. No doubt about it, having a woman in your life means you need to expect trouble around every corner. No way around it. I gotta say, though, the right woman is worth the trouble."

Having Zoey in his life would be worth any amount of trouble. Just as losing her when he'd just found her would suck beyond measure.

He remembered when they parted, him leaving for his shift, she staying to make her decision. She'd agreed to take some time to think it over. That was a week and a half ago. She'd even stayed in Connecticut for Thanksgiving. He'd been on duty on the holiday, so it wasn't like he'd been alone. He just had assumed she'd come back to the city. If not for him, at least for her business. But Zoey had suddenly developed the ability to stop worrying about that part of her life.

She said she'd spent Thanksgiving with her 'honorary aunts', whoever they were. She sounded really happy, too, which made Gordy very nervous.

Now here he was, giving her time to make a decision that could take her away from him. His heart clenched just at the thought.

Gordy was being amazingly well behaved, in his opinion, by not driving up there and trying to sway her decision. Not that he'd had time to drive back there between work, Santa School last week and then volunteering as Santa at the hospital on his days off this week.

He did call Zoey, though, every night before bed. It gave him great satisfaction that he was the last person she thought of before falling to sleep in that soft down-covered bed they'd shared for two brief nights.

He hadn't been this close to being happy in a while. Nor had he been this miserable. He sighed. *Women.*

"Yup." Scotty laughed and Gordy realized he'd said it aloud. Scot glanced over at him. "Hey, if you are all lovesick over some woman, what are you going to do when you get sold tomorrow night at the auction?"

Gordy groaned. "Thanks, another thing to worry about. I'd forgotten about that." He'd been so preoccupied with thoughts of Zoey moving away he hadn't even remembered to tell her about the calendar or the auction. It was just some trivial part of his life right now. Scotty was right, though. What was he going to do about it? Going out on a date, even for charity, with a woman who wasn't Zoey was the last thing Gordy wanted to do.

Gordy blew out a frustrated breath and continued to chop. "I'll figure something out. What are you going to do? You're with that Lexi Cooper yourself, aren't you? Isn't that the reason we've all been cooking for this damn thing, because you're getting laid by a famous chef and we all have to pay for it?"

"We are all cooking because it is a good cause and good publicity. My getting laid is just a fringe benefit," Scotty defended himself.

"Yeah, benefit for you maybe! All I'm getting out of it is practice chopping vegetables."

"To answer your question, Lexi is going to buy me. And you should be glad I'm not charging you for cooking lessons."

Gordy made a rude noise. "I don't need no stinking cooking lessons and you know it. Engine 31 eats just as well as Ladder 3, maybe better on the nights I cook." Gordy pointed at his own broad chest to emphasize the point.

Scotty raised a brow, knife paused above the green pepper on the cutting board. "You want to put your money where your mouth is?"

"What the hell is that supposed to mean?"

"A cook off," Scotty challenged.

Gordy scowled. "Judged by who? Your girlfriend? Yeah, that would be real fair."

"No, the guys from both houses, blind taste test so it's fair."

Gordy sighed. "Can we get through this auction crap first and talk about this contest later?" Like after he knew if he was losing the girl he might very well be in love with, he added to himself silently.

"You chicken of a little competition?"

"Chicken? No." Gordy shook his head. Pussy whipped?

Most definitely.

~

It was Friday when Zoey finally lost her mind. Over the last week and a half, she'd packed her aunt's clothes and donated them to charity. Organized the cabinets in the kitchen. Gone through all the old photo albums and cried until her eyes were bloodshot. Cooked for the aunts. Even read a book which she hadn't had time to do since opening her business. But the house that she loved so much had started to stifle her.

Cabin fever, was it called? Whatever it was, she missed the sounds of the city streets at night. She missed the never-ending phone calls and stream of people coming and going at the store. She missed Gordy, so much so it scared her. She'd tried staying away to give herself a real taste of what life would be like if she did actually close up shop and move to her aunt's house—make that her newly inherited house—permanently.

It taught her one thing—two actually. One, she was a city person at heart. This country stuff was fine for weekends or vacation, but not full time. Not for her. And two, she thrived on the hard work and pressure. Granted, too much pressure had made her believe she was having a heart attack, but a little pressure was good. It kept her on her toes.

So she'd said goodbye to the aunts with a promise to come back soon, packed her bag and took off. Driving back to her shop she ran all the pros and cons through her head again and it didn't matter which side of the list came up longer, she still came to the same conclusion, she didn't want to close Zoey's Events and retire to the country to bake cookies for the locals. Not yet anyway, maybe when she was sixty, or seventy.

She pulled up in front of the shop and found a parking space immediately. Taking that as a good omen, there was a renewed spring in her step as she pushed open the door and stopped dead in the doorway. The place was buzzing. Waiters in black and white uniforms zipped around carrying rentals and wrapped trays of food. Ralph and she counted one, two, three other chefs yelled orders and last minute instructions all while she stood there dumbstruck.

Ralph finally saw her and made his way through the crowd, and it was a crowd, to get to her. "Zoey! Why didn't you tell me you were coming home?"

He stopped with the cheerful greeting when he saw the expression on her face. "Okay, you're surprised. That's fine. I can explain."

She raised a brow. "Okay. Go ahead." Secretly, she wondered if Ralph had staged some sort of coup and now owned Zoey's without her. She had left him to himself for a long while.

Ralph spoke rapidly. "I took on more jobs so I could take on more employees. Well, actually, it was the other way around. When I took on more employees, I realized I could take on more jobs and still turn a profit for you. So when Lexi Cooper left a message saying that she needed staff for her fundraiser and asked if I could recommend any waiters or a Sous Chef…"

"You stepped right up."

Ralph grinned. "Damn right. It's Lexi Cooper!"

"Did she also tell you she's paying cost of goods because it's for charity?"

"Oh, we're not doing the food. She got the firemen to do that. We're just supplying staffing and she's paying them. On top of that, she listed us in the program for free just for helping her out! That's going to be great advertising. Apparently there's a shortage of caterers and wait staff at the moment. She was happy I could help at all."

Zoey glanced around. "How did you get so many?"

"I put a sign up in the bar." He grinned.

"Do they have any experience?"

"Well, I wouldn't have them doing French service at The Ritz but yeah, they've all waited tables before. I mean, really, who hasn't, right? And it's just passed hors d'oeuvres and stations tonight. Not a sit down dinner or anything."

"And the job I had already scheduled for tonight?"

"That was a simple gig. One of the interns is going to do it. That's what all this food and the rentals are for."

"We have interns now," Zoey said flatly.

"Yeah!" Then Ralph noticed she was not happy and paused. "You're not mad at me, are you Zoe?"

Zoey shrugged.

"Look. I have this whole great plan and I even printed out a business proposal for you. We can make this work, Zoey. Just like Gordy said. With your creativity and my business sense, we'll be as big as Lexi Cooper!"

"Gordy said that?"

"Yeah. He's the one that gave me the idea to propose a partnership to you. I just wanted to wait for you to get home before I approached you with it."

She tried but couldn't help the smile that crept onto her lips as she shook her head. "Have you seen him today?"

"Gordy? No. Not today. Actually, not the last few days."

She'd called him on the drive but got no answer. Disappointed, she decided to do what she did best, throw herself into work. "Do I have a clean chef's jacket here?"

Ralph's face lit up. "You're going to help?"

"Sure. Why not? I'll go to the first gig with our new intern, make sure he's set up and the customer is happy, then I'll meet you at Lexi's party. It will be an experience working with Lexi Cooper anyway. I can add it to my resume."

Ralph laughed. "She should be adding working with you to her own resume. We have to get over there...and look how convenient, you parked right in front. I'll have the food for the other party loaded into your car."

He rounded up the staff and had them and the food loaded into the cars like he'd been managing staff forever. Then, they were all off to their various assignments.

Chapter 8

Gordy realized that getting through the auction crap wasn't going to be so easy. Not one little bit and not only for him.

"Shit. How many do you see?" Troy O'Donnell asked from his hiding spot behind a large leafy potted plant.

"I'm not sure. At least half a dozen. You have to look yourself, Troy. How am I supposed to recognize all the women you used to sleep with? It's not as if you branded them or anything." Antonio threw his hands up in frustration and backed up to join Troy behind the plant.

Scotty laughed. "Certified TC—Troy's Choice."

Troy scowled at his suggestion for an appropriate brand and dared a look at the crowd himself. "Shit. I count a dozen. Oh, great. There's one standing right next to my fiancé…and they're chatting." Troy groaned. "I am so screwed."

Troy's sister, the photographer, was suddenly beside them. She lowered her camera and shook her head. "Told you. You should have warned Amy before tonight that there could be a few ex-girlfriends here bidding on you."

"Thanks, Tessa. An 'I told you so' is exactly what I need right now." Troy crossed his arms across his naked chest. She raised her camera again and said, "Smile."

A string of foul language that would have cost Troy about a twenty for the Engine 31 cuss jar met Tessa's suggestion.

Gordy took the opportunity and did some peeking himself to make sure his own plan was in place. After getting a look at these women, all circling in wait like hungry sharks, he knew for absolute certainty that he did not want to be bought tonight by any one of them.

He glanced around at the dozen bachelors for sale and realized how funny they all looked waiting for the public auction about to start on the stage set up on Bryant's third floor.

Twelve firemen, shirtless, wearing nothing but fire pants and boots as Troy's sister ran around taking pictures to capture their embarrassment for posterity. The owner of Bryant's, Jason Bryant himself, glided through the event with his assistant, checking the sound system and last minute details.

Gordy saw Scotty wave at his girlfriend Lexi Cooper as she zipped around behind the scenes, cleaning up the remains of the cocktail party. Scotty was safe, Lexi was going to buy him.

Antonio had nothing to worry about either, Gordy remembered as he saw Antonio waving at a blonde woman.

"That your girl?" Gordy asked.

Antonio nodded. "Maddie. She and the women from her law firm are chipping in to buy me. They're going to share me at the firm's holiday party and make me dance with them all." He laughed and shrugged. "There are worse things, I guess."

Troy snorted. "Yeah, tell me about it."

Gordy sighed. He certainly hoped his own safety net didn't fall through. With Zoey still in Connecticut, he'd had to make alternate plans to keep his own virtue safe from the throngs of women.

He had the sudden urge to call Zoey, but he'd left his cell phone in the car. He sighed. Oh, well. Once this gig was over he was driving out there and cementing the fact that he was a part of her life, no matter what decision she eventually made.

That resolve in mind, he braced himself as the music started and Jason Bryant took his place as announcer behind the podium.

"Here we go, boys. Good luck." Gordy hiked his pants up a bit higher over his naked torso and moved closer to the stage as Jason called Mr. January up first. Being Mr. February, Gordy would be up next. As the women screamed Gordy blew out a breath hoping that as Mr. February, Cupid would be on his side not only for this auction, but with Zoey, too.

~

Zoey rode the escalator from the parking lot to the restaurant level at Bryant's Department Store. She'd set up the other party and then left the intern at the other job, confident that all was well, but it had taken her forever to get across town and then find a parking space.

By the time she arrived in the Bryant's kitchen, everyone was cleaning up and wrapping the leftovers.

"Guess I missed it," she said when she found Ralph.

He grinned at her. "You may have missed the cocktail party, but you are just in time for the main event."

She frowned. "What are you talking about? Cocktails for five hundred wasn't the main event?"

Ralph shook his head. "Oh, no." He reached into his duffle bag and pulled out a calendar. "Look what I bought for you today."

He handed it to her and she glanced down. "A fireman calendar?"

"Take a look at Mr. February."

She flipped to the page and her eyes grew wide.

Ralph laughed. "And that's not all. The calendar men are being auctioned off upstairs any minute." He grabbed her arm. "Come on. We have to get up there."

She pulled back. Gordy hadn't mentioned the calendar to her. Why? And now he was being auctioned off and had kept the whole thing secret?

"What's wrong?" Ralph paused.

She swallowed. "Um, nothing. Let's go on up."

From the escalator she could hear the announcer and women cheering. By the time they got even near the stage Gordy was already down the runway and on his return trip. She heard the announcer over the microphone. "Five hundred dollars. Do I hear six?"

Ralph grabbed her arm. "You have to buy him!"

She shook her head. It was true that with her recent inheritance she was no longer in danger of being destitute and homeless, but if Gordy had wanted her to buy him, surely he would have told her about the auction. The fact that he didn't made her wonder what exactly their relationship was. Two days of great sex and over a week's worth of nightly phone calls had led her to assume they were well on their way to being a couple. But now…

"Why not?" Ralph demanded.

She just shook her head again and watched as the bids rose until the announcer finally slammed the gavel against the podium and said, "Sold for one thousand dollars to the lovely lady in pink."

She saw Gordy smile broadly at the winning bidder and her heart fell. Zoey steeled her nerves and dared to look at the woman who'd made him so happy and then frowned. Gordy had pulled a frail elderly woman up the stairs and walked with her back behind the stage.

For the first time since Ralph had told her about this auction she felt she could breath again. She still didn't know why he hadn't told her about this whole thing but one thing was clear, Gordy wasn't cheating on her with the lovely lady in pink.

She looked up at Ralph. "I'm going in back to find Gordy."

He nodded. "I'm going to stay up here and watch the rest of the guys get humiliated so I can tease them next time they're in the bar."

Leaving Ralph to his fun, she worked her way back passed the podium until she found where the men were stashed behind a few folding screens and potted plants.

Gordy spotted her, smiled and was next to her in a few strides. She didn't even have time to say hello because his mouth covered hers in an instant. She sunk into those big teddy bear arms of his, swearing to herself that she'd never allow him to let go.

He finally broke the kiss, smiling again. "You're back."

She nodded. "For good."

His eyes opened wide. "You're not moving and closing your business?"

Zoey shook her head and laughed. "No. Country life is

not for me. I guess I'm a city girl. Besides, I don't think Ralph would let me close up the shop even if I wanted to. I seem to have a new partner."

Gordy blushed a bit. "I think I might have had a little something to do with that."

Zoey noticed the woman who'd bought Gordy trying to get their attention. "I think your new owner wants you."

Gordy grinned. "Come meet her."

Zoey was pulled over to the woman and introduced. "Rose, this is my girlfriend Zoey. Zoey, this is my neighbor Rose."

Zoey smiled from being called his girlfriend and extended a hand to Rose. "Nice to meet you."

"Very nice to finally meet you, too. Gordy does nothing but talk about you. Zoey this and Zoey that. I'm glad you're back." Rose turned to Gordy. "I'm going to go. I'll see you soon?"

"Yes ma'am, on my next day off. I'll stop by the paint store with those chips you picked out."

She nodded, said her goodbyes and left.

Zoey frowned. "What was that about?"

Gordy grinned. "I made a deal with her. She buys me and I paint her entire apartment. She got an estimate from a painter for two grand so I'd say she got herself a bargain and the children's hospital gets a thousand more dollars."

Zoey smiled at the big hunk who was the sweetest guy in the world. "I'd say she did get herself quite a deal, but why didn't you tell me about this? I would have bought you, too, you know. And not for painting, either."

He shrugged. "You can have *that* for free. Besides, you had a lot on your mind lately, and I'd rather have you spending your money on things like health insurance."

She nodded. "I will, lots of things will be different at work from now on, I think. But right now, the best health insurance I can think of would be borrowing you from Rose and going back to my apartment." She raised a suggestive brow.

He groaned and kissed her hard. "Oh, sweetie. I can think of nothing better. But hold onto to that thought for just a few more minutes, just until we reach Mr. December. I think it's going to be worth seeing."

Gordy explained his friend Troy's sticky situation to her as the crowd of screaming women continued to bid on month after month of half naked calendar men.

They watched his friend Scott, Mr. July go up and get snatched up by none other than Miss Lexi Cooper herself, who apparently was his girlfriend. They waited through a few more months until Gordy's other friend Antonio, Mr. October, was purchased by a group of women who, she was told, were going to share him. Finally, November was finished and Troy was up, looking like he was headed for the gallows.

His fear proved valid as the bidding went wild. Women from every corner of the room stepped forward, yelling bids at the wide-eyed announcer. The photographer stopped snapping photos and stood next to them to watch, looking pretty in shock herself.

Gordy quickly introduced her as Mr. December's sister Tessa.

When the bids reached four thousand dollars Gordy blew out a breath. "This is bad."

Troy's sister Tessa shook her head. "Worse than bad. I have to do something." She took off running and caught the attention of the announcer. He hissed something quickly back to Tessa, who then took off in another direction as he went back to announcing the still growing bids.

Zoey glanced at the woman Gordy had pointed out as Troy's fiancé. She'd dropped out of the bidding and was starting to look very concerned and more than a bit confused.

Suddenly, an older woman with dark hair and striking eyebrows stood up on a display, right next to a mini-skirt clad mannequin and announced loud and clear, "Ten thousand dollars!"

The announcer smiled at her. "Ten thousand dollars for

Mr. December. I don't think we can do much better than that, folks. Sold! Let's give the winning bidder a hand." The crowd cheered, all except for the losing bidders, as the announcer banged the gavel. "Thank you to all the bidders."

Troy shot the announcer a look that said 'thank you for saving my life' and was visibly relieved as he left the stage.

"What just happened?" Zoey asked.

Gordy smiled. "The announcer is Jason Bryant, as in the Bryant family, owners of this store and rich as you can get. He's dating Troy's sister and the woman who just bid is his assistant. Apparently, Jason just saved Troy's ass and Troy owes him big time."

Zoey shook her head. "I'd say so. This is way too complicated. But I have to say, it's far better than sitting in the country watching the frost on the windows melt. This is the most excitement I've had in a long time."

Gordy leaned down and kissed her. "Let's get out of here and I'll see if I can beat it."

"I know you can, especially if we stop by my shop on the way and pick up some whipped cream."

He raised a brow. "And chocolate sauce?"

She laughed. "Sure, as long as there's no penis cookies."

"Hey, I hold a very special place in my heart for penis cookies. They brought us together, remember?"

"Yes, I do remember." Fate worked in strange ways.

Gordy asked, "Do you think your aunt made penis cookies for her cookie company in Connecticut?"

Zoey considered. You never knew with Aunt Zoe. "I honestly don't know. I'll have to ask the aunts. I wish you could have met her. I think she would have loved you, Gordy, as much as I do."

She hadn't meant to say it, but there it was, hanging in the air. She glanced at him nervously.

Gordy paused and turned toward her. He held her chin in one hand and kissed her, right there in the middle of Bryant's Department Store as women leaving the auction streamed passed them. "I love you, too, Zoey."

At that moment it didn't matter where they were or whom they were with, or even that Gordy was wearing nothing more than fireman pants. They were together and all was right with the world.

The End

About the Author:

It all started in first grade when Cat Johnson won the essay contest at Hawthorne Elementary School and got to ride in the Chief of Police's car in the Memorial Day Parade…and the rest, as they say, is history. As an adult, Cat generally tries to stay out of police cars and is thrilled to be writing for a living. She has been published under a different name in the Young Adult genre, but Linden Bay is the first to release her romances.

On a personal note, Cat has two horses, 10 cats, one dog, six parakeets, numerous fish and one husband, and is not sure which of those gives her the most grief. Needless to say, she is very busy most days on her little 18th century farm in New York State. She plays the harp professionally and stresses that this does not mean she plays well. A past bartender, marketing manager and Junior League president, Cat's life is quite the dichotomy, and on any given day she is just as likely to be in formal eveningwear as in mucking clothes covered in manure. Cat hates the telephone but loves email, and is looking forward to hearing from you.

cat.johnson@lindenbayromance.com

Other works by Cat Johnson:

Trilogy No. 102: Opposites Attract

...a three-part lighthearted romp through the intertwining lives of six people who learn that in spite of everything you have to remember to live, love and laugh to be happy.

Taking a Leap: Bradley Morgan is the quintessential computer geek and nice guy, through and through. The only problem is that in his opinion, nice guys almost always finish last when it comes to hot women like his sexy co-worker Alyssa Jones. But things change after Alyssa finds her boyfriend cheating. Suddenly, nice guys like Brad don't look so bad. So when Brad agrees to ghostwrite the sex scenes for a romance novel as a favor for desperate client Maria White and asks for Alyssa's help after hours, she agrees wholeheartedly and things really start to heat up. Brad and Alyssa learn you should never judge a book by its cover, and that sometimes love requires a leap of faith.

Light my Fire: Amy Gerald's life is filled with whirlwind romance. Unfortunately, it's all on the pages of the romance novels she publishes. That is until she volunteers to cat-sit for her author friend Maria and meets Troy O'Donnell, the hunky fireman who lives next door. The problem is, this commitment-phobic consummate bachelor is far more willing to run into a burning building than allow love into his life. Troy will grasp at any excuse, even the ridiculous assumption that Amy is a lesbian, just to avoid his growing feelings for her. Amid a comedy of errors and misunderstandings, which includes Troy's first hilarious visit to a gay bar, Amy manages to light Troy's fire, but can she also conquer his fears?

Second Time Around: Antonio Sanchez thought that at 32 his life was all mapped out—wife, kids, career...until some major bumps in the road radically alter his course and send him careening right into the path of newly divorced Maddie Morgan. Suddenly thrust back into single life, Antonio moves back in with his old-fashioned parents and has to learn to juggle his kids, his job at the firehouse, and his role as Best Man for his newly engaged best friend Troy, all in addition to facing his unquenchable desire for Maddie. Throw in a slew of matchmaking friends and relatives, led by Maria whose apartment appears to be the Bermuda Triangle for lost lovers, and Antonio and Maddie discover just how complicated things can get. Can the pair prove that love really is better the second time around?

Trilogy No. 103: Red Hot & Blue

Trey: Special operative Trey Williams doesn't want a girlfriend, nor does he need one in his life. A distracted soldier is a dead soldier, that's his motto. The problem is, the woman who has been recruited to pose as his wife on a special assignment is proving to be more of a distraction than Trey can handle. What's a soldier to do?

Jack: Ordered by his superiors to take time off for his "mental health", Jack Gordon heads back to his hometown for two weeks of R&R. But then he meets Nicki Camp, the new hand his brother has just hired to help out at the family farm. Is Nicki playing hard to get, or is she hiding something? Jack knows one thing...he isn't going to rest until he finds out!

Jimmy: Jimmy Gordon has learned during his career in the Special Forces that he can handle pretty much anything, including pretending to be everything from a banquet waiter to a terrorist, while undercover. But there is one thing he finds he's having a bit of difficulty handling, and that's the governor's hot red-headed daughter, Amelia Monroe-Carrington. Maybe the time for pretending is over?

Trilogy No. 105: Smalltown, U.S.A. by Cat Johnson

*You loved Pigeon Hollow in **Trilogy No. 103: Red Hot & Blue**. Now, really get to know the men of this quintessential Smalltown, U.S.A.*

The Horseman: Jared Gordon considers himself a lucky man. He enjoys the simple things life has to offer: a slice of his mama's pie, a pretty girl, a well-bred horse. Life on his farm in Pigeon Hollow is good, until big city girl Mandy Morris blows into town. Like a tornado hitting a trailer park, Mandy turns Jared's simple life upside down. Will he ever be the same again?

The Ballplayer: Cole Ryan found a life of fame and fortune in the major leagues. When an injury takes him out of the game he returns to Pigeon Hollow, the small town he thought he'd left behind. Yet every cloud has a silver lining, and for Cole that would be returning to the arms of Lizzie Barton, the smalltown girl who got away a decade ago and still haunts his dreams. Will the secret she's been hiding from him all these years get in the way of their future?

The Deputy: Deputy Sheriff Bobby Barton agreed to put up with the taping of a reality TV show in his town for two reasons. He thought it would be good for the town's business, and the producers promised they'd keep out of his. But the show keeps creeping into his personal life, and he finds himself hoping that the show's assistant producer, Christy Dunne, would creep into his bed. Did Deputy Barton make a mistake that will cost him his heart?

This is a publication of

Linden Bay Romance

WWW.LINDENBAYROMANCE.COM

Recommended Linden Bay Romance Read:

Trilogy No. 101: Turning Up The Heat

You just never know where you're going to find love....

Blackout: Ashley and Curt get trapped together in an elevator. As the temperature rises they begin to reveal themselves in more ways then one!

Touch the Fire: Firefighter Garrett Flint rescues the beautiful Nicole from a burning building and then breaks all the rules by taking her into his home and into his heart.

June in August: June Monroe grew up next door to Wiley Patton. When he left for Vietnam she was just fifteen and hopelessly in love. Now three years later he's returned from war and little June is all grown up.

623688

Made in the USA